T0209259

Warrior of the World

Books by Jeffe Kennedy

Warrior of the World

Jeffe Kennedy

REBEL BASE BOOKS
Kensington Publishing Corp.
www.kensingtonbooks.com

Rebel Base Books are published by
Kensington Publishing Corp. 119 West 40th Street New York, NY 10018

All Kensington titles, imprints, and distributed lines are available at special quantity discounts for bulk purchases for sales promotion, premiums, fundraising, and educational or institutional use.

To the extent that the image or images on the cover of this book depict a person or persons, such person or persons are merely models, and are not intended to portray any character or characters featured in the book.

Special book excerpts or customized printings can also be created to fit specific needs. For details, write or phone the office of the Kensington Special Sales Manager:
Kensington Publishing Corp.
119 West 40th Street
New York, NY 10018
Attn. Special Sales Department. Phone: 1-800-221-2647.

First Electronic Edition: January 2019
ISBN-13: 978-1-63573-042-5 (ebook)
ISBN-10: 1-63573-042-2 (ebook)

First Print Edition: January 2019
ISBN-13: 978-1-63573-045-6
ISBN-10: 1-63573-045-7

Printed in the United States of America

For Sarah,
Who talked me out of my tree and
is the reason this particular story exists.

Acknowledgments

Many thanks to the folks who read this story with a short turn-around and gave me terrific insights on how to round off this trilogy: Marcella Burnard, Jim Sorenson, and Sage Walker.

A huge thank you to Lauren Vassallo, Communications Manager at Rebel Base Books, for her inventive and tireless marketing support—and for telling me the books made her cry and miss her subway stop.

Thanks to Tara Gavin for acquiring this trilogy and giving me the opportunity to tell this particular side-tale, and to all the Rebel Base Team. Appreciation and gratitude to Rebecca Cremonese for pulling miracles out of the fire time and again. Yes, I know that's a mixed metaphor. I dare you to fix it.

Hello and thanks to all the folks who hang in the SFWA Slack chat room. You all brighten my days, and your friendship and encouragement mean everything.

Thanks to my mom, who tries *really hard* not to text me when she knows I'm writing. Hooray for new hips!

Shout out to Minerva Spencer for fantastic support on this trilogy, too. And, while I'm at it, the Land of Enchantment Romance Authors (LERA) for always applauding.

Hugs, kisses, and martinis to Sarah Younger: fantastic agent, cheerleader, and dispenser of publishing wisdom. You're the best!

Love to Carien, who always has the best snark for my whining – and who also cried at these books.

And to David, first and last, who is always there.

Prologue

I was an Imperial Princess of Dasnaria and I grew up in paradise.

Tropically warm, lushly beautiful, replete with luxury, my childhood world was without flaw. My least whim was met with immediate indulgence, served instantly and with smiles of delight. My siblings and I spent our days in play, nothing ever asked or expected of us.

Until the day everything was demanded—and taken—from me.

Only then did I finally see our paradise for what it was, how deliberately designed to mold and shape us. A breeding ground for luxurious accessories. To create a work of art, you grow her in an environment of elegance and beauty. To make her soft and lusciously accommodating, you surround her with delicacies and everything delightful. And you don't educate her in anything but being pleasing.

Education leads to critical thinking, not a desirable trait in a princess of Dasnaria, thus I was protected from anything that might taint the virginity of my mind as well as my body.

Because I'd understood so little of the world outside, when my time came to be plucked from the garden, when the snip of the shears severed me from all I'd known, the injury came as a shock so devastating that I had no ability to even understand what it meant, much less summon the will to resist and overcome. Which, I've also come to realize over time, was also a part of the deliberate design.

I wish I could take credit for extracting myself from the brutal horror of the marriage they forced me into, but I can't. If not for my baby brother Harlan, I would've continued through the harsh winter of my wedding journey, my physical and emotional injuries muted by the numbing teas and smoke they supplied me with, and inevitably to worse torture and eventual death.

But Harlan broke me out and we escaped. Miraculously, I even made it onto a sailing ship, bound for a greater world I knew nothing about, while Harlan remained behind, a captive of our ruthless family.

Even then, I likely couldn't have survived on my own. Full of fear and ignorance, I barely left my cabin, having no idea what I might do with myself. Until Kaja, Warrior Priestess of Danu, coaxed and then forced me to face my future. She taught me to defend myself. She gave me a disguise and vows of chastity and silence to protect me from discovery.

She gave me my self back again.

And Ochieng… He gave me stories, a home, and my heart's desire.

Without these people, I couldn't have survived. But I can't be the helpless kept princess all my life. At some point I need to find the warrior in myself.

If only I knew how.

~ 1 ~

Despite the rain, I went to see the elephants. Especially Efe.

In the endless downpour, it hardly mattered what I put on. Whatever it was became soaked within moments. I'd finally adopted the habit of the Nyamburans, wearing light fabrics that at least didn't hang on me like iron manacles with the weight of all that water. When I returned to the house, I'd then hang them next to one of the fired clay stoves, switching them out for another set.

It gave me an excuse to sit quietly and try to recover my strength—and wind—while hanging onto my pride. Perhaps I fooled no one with my attentiveness to drying my clothes.

Especially as nothing ever seemed to dry completely. Even Ochieng's elaborate descriptions hadn't done the rainy season justice. It poured nonstop, day and night. Below the granite butte the D'tiembo house perched upon, the river swelled until it seemed to fill the entire valley. No longer shining bright like a polished sword, it lay gray and sullen, deceptively still—until debris sweeping downstream revealed the lethal currents that tumbled them past, a great beast masticating its treasures as it carried them away.

Though I felt naked without my leathers, I'd given them up as too impractical in the pervasive damp. I'd even stopped wearing the vambraces, which had always been more to cover up the scars on my wrists from my wedding bracelets. I wouldn't say I no longer cared who saw them, but they were certainly no longer secret. All the D'tiembos knew what I came from and what had happened to me. Another reason not to bother with pride, though I couldn't seem to help myself.

There seemed to be very little I could control about myself. I hadn't picked up my knives and sword since I'd returned either.

I didn't trust myself with a sharp weapon.

Slipping out of my little room, I left the sodden curtains hanging in place instead of tying them back, so it wouldn't be obvious I wasn't within. Though I'd given up my vow of silence—and of chastity, though I'd yet to do anything there beyond giving up the silver disk of the promise—I didn't often feel like talking to people. You'd think I'd have a lot of words dammed up inside me, like the debris in the river fighting to race to the sea, but once I'd told Ochieng my story, I didn't seem to have much left to say.

Or, more precisely, nothing I felt comfortable articulating. Back to that pride. The legacy of my mother, a curse I perversely treasured for its cool familiarity.

I'd killed Rodolf, my now late husband, in a blur of blood and violence I barely remembered. But that hadn't killed the hatred he'd planted in me. As my body healed from that brutal battle, all of my fear and pain gained life again, too. Sometimes it overcame me, the rage-terror, the many-faced emotion that flashed like a fire no amount of rain could quench. Sometimes I thought another person lived inside me. Perhaps Imperial Princess Jenna, daughter of Empress Hulda, the most ruthless bitch in the Dasnarian Empire, hadn't become Ivariel. I might have created Ivariel, Warrior Priestess of Danu, but she only provided a calm shell over the dark face of Jenna.

Jenna, who couldn't seem to stop hating, and whom I couldn't seem to control.

The antechamber was empty, as usual, since my room sat on a less-frequented edge of the many-tiered house, and I moved silently through it and down the woven grass steps few people besides me used, suppressing a groan at the aching protest of my body. Amazing how simple movements like going down steps made my abdomen protest and my always-strong legs tremble with weakness. I thought I'd endured pain before and understood it. Had conquered it.

But those had been mostly surface pains—from flogging and my late husband's rough attentions. Mostly skin deep, except in my woman's passage, which was meant to open to the outside anyway. These wounds had penetrated through layers of tissue and muscle and organs, deep inside me, hindering my smallest movements. Pointed reminders that I should be dead.

With determination, ignoring the pain, I descended the slow steps to the terrace. When I'd arrived, in the dry season, the large D'tiembo clan had spent most of their time on the big, low-walled terrace that overlooked the river. These days it mostly held puddles of rainwater. One of my young students, Ayela, and her brother, Femi, used long-handled tools to push water that collected in the corners and deeper indentations over the edge of the terrace. It seemed like an exercise in futility to me, but all the kids took turns doing it. Maybe to keep them occupied as much as anything.

Ayela spotted me and waved, a cautious gesture, her normal ebullience carefully muted. They were all careful with me. I could hardly blame them. She and my other students were anxious, I knew, to resume lessons with me. I also knew their parents had spoken firmly with them that they should not ask me, that I needed time to get strong again. The first eighteen years of my life had been spent in the seraglio of the Imperial Palace where the ladies all honed eavesdropping to a fine art. The D'tiembos with their curtain walls and privacy that existed only via courtesy could hardly keep secrets from me.

I smiled at Ayela, but quickly turned away so she wouldn't get the wrong idea. If only I could go down the cliff steps. However—exactly as Ochieng had predicted—the lower levels had been swept away, even before I managed to escape my sickbed for the first time. So, I went around, skirting the edge of the terrace rather than going through the house, making my way to the back side, where the covered steps descended to the storehouses.

"Ivariel." Ochieng stepped out from a room I passed, his lean face smooth, his dark eyes full of concern. "Going to visit the elephants?" he asked.

I nodded, then remembered I should give him words, since he seemed to crave them from me. "Yes. Is that all right?"

A slight line formed between his brows. "Of course. This is your home. You may do anything you wish. I simply thought to offer to go with you."

"You don't have to," I replied, my gaze going to the opening leading to the steps. I'd been so close. "I'm sure you have other things to do."

He laughed, though not in a genuine way. "It's the rainy season. Nobody has anything to do that they haven't done dozens of times already. I'll go with you."

Because it felt churlish and ungenerous of me to refuse, I nodded and continued walking, Ochieng falling in beside me. "How are you feeling today?" he asked me.

I never knew how to answer this question. "Better," I said, as I usually did. Not an untruth—I certainly felt better than I had when I first awoke in the D'tiembo home, swathed in bandages, with no idea why I was there instead of dead. One day I wanted to feel again as I had before my eighteenth birthday, before any of this occurred. I missed feeling limber, vital, and beautiful. I hadn't appreciated what a blessing those things were when I had them. Now that I would value them as precious gifts, I suspected I'd lost those, too, forever.

"You're moving less stiffly," Ochieng observed. We reached the steps going down the rock face, and I clung to the hand rail. At least here the grass roof kept most of the rain off. The steps, also woven of dried and cured grasses, acted like a sieve, so water didn't collect on them. They gave slightly under our weight, though, which made my internal muscles clench painfully as they worked to keep me balanced. Keenly aware that Ochieng watched me, I tried my best not to show it.

He, his mother, Zalaika, and all the D'tiembo clan—but mostly those two—had taken great care of me, nursing me back to health. I had nothing but gratitude for their diligence and yet… Perhaps I was not a person who did gratitude well.

"I was thinking," Ochieng continued, moving far slower than his usual athletic speed, pacing himself to match my measured progress, "that it might be good for you to practice your martial forms again. Easy movements, to build up your strength." And confidence, he didn't say, but my mind supplied the words.

"They're really just dances," I replied, aware of the flat resistance in my voice. "I told you that. I'm a dancer, nothing more. Kaja—" My voice broke on her name. I'd found out about Kaja's death only moments before the warning arrived, on the same caravan, as if they carried all the terrible news in one of their wagons, that my late husband's men had followed me all the way to Nyambura. I hadn't had time to properly mourn her, wasn't even sure what form that might take. Losing her felt like yet another deep-dwelling wound, one that ached, swamping me with misery at odd times.

Ochieng set a hand on the small of my back, a brief touch, and I realized I'd stopped. "We could visit the elephants later," he said softly.

"No." I resumed walking, ignoring his almost inaudible sigh for my stubbornness. I might've lied when I said "better." Yesterday's descent had been easier than today's so far. It made no sense, why some days my body hurt more than others. But ever since I first made it down the steps to see Efe, Violet, and the other elephants, I'd made sure to go every day. Even if it ended up being the only thing I did all day. Which it often was, particularly after the long ascent. "Anyway, I know I told you—they're not really martial forms. Kaja taught me to hold a weapon while I did the dances I already knew, because she didn't have time to teach me the real stuff. I'm not really a Warrior Priestess of Danu at all. Nothing like she was."

He let that go, as he had every time I brought it up. "Dances, then. Maybe it's time to try those."

"It's too rainy."

"We can make a space inside."

We finally reached the storehouse level, where the rain sheeted off the grass sheaves at the top of the immense three-story structure. People waved to us and called greetings. They tended the small fires distributed throughout to keep the damp from setting into the stored goods. Hart, who'd traveled on the *Robin* with us from Ehas, called a hello to me as we passed. He was using a long pick to sift the big piles of hay, airing the stuff so it didn't mold. Earning his keep, as I was not.

I stopped at the bins of fruit, selecting some favorites for my girls.

"Ochieng," I said, as soon as we were alone again. "I don't want to dance."

"Why not?" He sounded genuinely curious. "Can you explain to me?"

I couldn't. The thought of even trying made me feel weary. More than the physical exhaustion of just getting to ground level. The red soil had become thick mud, carved into channels of fast-flowing streams. Barefoot, I stepped off the platform into it, sinking up to my ankles, feeling as if it would suck me down entirely. And I still had to go back up again.

Efe had spotted me though. She'd been waiting for me to appear, and came galloping through the rain, waving her trunk in the air in elephantine celebration. She slowed as she reached me, wrapping her trunk gently around my head in her version of an embrace. Efe and I had started a friendship before the battle where I killed my late husband, but since then we seemed to have developed a special bond.

Ochieng had told me that Efe had insisted on coming with them when the D'tiembo fighters mounted up to rescue me, though she wasn't trained for battle. Rescued only a year before, and a difficult case, Efe resisted training. Even Ochieng, the master trainer, hadn't been able to cling to her back for more than a few moments. When they'd rallied and equipped the fighting elephants, they'd tried to make her stay back, but short of restraining her—which they'd never do, particularly to Efe—they couldn't persuade her. She came with the others and she'd found me, then curled around my back while I thought I lay dying, dreaming of elephants thundering around me.

I knew in my head that Ochieng, the D'tiembos, and the battle elephants had saved me, but in my heart, it had been Efe.

She started dragging at me, pulling me toward the elephant shelter and out of the rain. Efe didn't much like the constant downpour, hunching in it miserably as if it attacked her. I went along, largely because when an elephant decides she'd like you to go somewhere, you went, but also because I liked it in the elephant shelter, out of the rain and pressed in with the big beasts. Ochieng naturally came along, greeted with enthusiasm by Violet and the others.

Efe snaked her trunk over me, whuffling and sniffing until she found the fruit I'd stuck in my pockets. I rescued a melon for Violet, who plucked it from my hand with all the grave dignity befitting the matriarch, then let Efe root out the rest. With a happy sigh, I felt myself relax. Ochieng glanced at me, raising his brows, inviting me to speak.

"I feel good here," I told him. "That's part of why I want to come visit the elephants, even though it's difficult for me."

He nodded. "And the dancing?"

The thought of even trying to dance—or picking up a blade—had my stomach clenching. So I lifted a shoulder and let it fall in a Dasnarian shrug of dismissal.

"You know." Ochieng had picked up a brush, circling it over Violet's broad forehead, and she closed her eyes in ecstasy. "I used to think that if you could only speak, I'd understand you better."

"And now?" I made myself ask.

He glanced at me over his shoulder. "Now I wonder if I'll ever understand you at all."

~ 2 ~

I turned back to Efe, who expected nothing from me. "I never asked you to understand me."

He didn't answer immediately. Then he came over and stood behind me, arms braced on Efe's big flank on either side of me where I leaned into her comforting bulk. He didn't touch me, but his warmth crossed the small space between us, his breath whispering against my temple.

"Fair enough," he said quietly. Oh so quietly, as if we might be overheard and he wanted the words to be only for me. "Understanding you is something *I* want. You fascinate me, Ivariel. From the first moment I saw you aboard the *Robin*, I was drawn to you—not just for your extraordinary beauty, but by something deeper. You were unlike any woman I'd seen before, and I wanted to *know* you. Perhaps I imagined more into your silence than there was, but I thought we'd become friends."

I leaned into Efe, listening, almost holding my breath, uncertain if delight or dread had me agonizing over what the next moments would bring. Ochieng had never declared himself to me, not in so many words, though he had kissed me. Twice. Here I had no fathers or brothers for him to approach and negotiate with, to seal my wedding vows with. In truth, I had no idea how the Nyamburans handled such things at all.

"That morning you woke up," he continued, after I said nothing, "you gave me the disk with your vow of chastity. Do you want it back?"

Of course he would've saved it, probably keeping it with the other disk for my forsaken vow of silence. I didn't have Kaja—or anyone of Danu—to ask, but I felt sure those vows given to Danu, once broken, couldn't be easily taken up again. Certainly I had no temple to visit, no altar to swear upon. My vows had never been meant to last forever, regardless. Silence had kept my accent and poor fluency disguised. Chastity had been a protection of another kind.

"You must prepare to be courted," Kaja had said. And then, *"I think that you do not wish to engage in such activities. Not yet. Maybe not ever."* Maybe not ever.

The memory of those words dug into my heart now as much as they had then.

"Ivariel?" Ochieng made a question of my name. "Do you want it back?" I shook my head.

"Can you use words to talk to me about this then?" He asked, his voice a little rough. "I know silence is a safe place for you, but I need to know what you're thinking, what you need from me."

I'd been cowardly, avoiding him, taking refuge in not speaking and staying alone in my room. He'd respected that—and likely would forever—but it wasn't fair. He was wrong about that. Screwing up my courage, I turned, tucking my hands behind my back and carefully not touching him, Efe solid against my back, but facing him. I couldn't quite make myself look into his eyes—old habits die hard and that one seemed to be one that fought to remain—so I focused on his mouth, his full lips.

But that made me think of when he'd kissed me, and I couldn't be thinking of that, and all the crazy ways it had made me feel, for this conversation.

So I looked at his throat, the strong column of it dark against his open white shirt, and the tender dip where the skin paled a little above the wings of his collarbones and between the fork of his neck tendons. The impulse to press my lips there, to taste his skin, to burrow into the warmth and comfort he offered unsettled me. I both wanted and didn't want.

"When I was a girl," I told him, "I always knew I would marry when I turned eighteen, that my father would pick a husband for me. I never questioned that—or that I would give my body to my husband without reserve to use as he pleased."

Ochieng made a sound, and his throat worked as he swallowed, but he didn't say anything because I plunged on.

"And from that union, I would have babies. I wanted children." My eyes flicked up to his dark ones, and away again. "I think… not only because it was my duty and destiny to carry on the imperial line. Somewhere in me, I still want that. I know that I'm unwilling—" Unaccountably my voice shook and broke there, the rage welling up in a sharp sweep. "I refuse to let my late husband ruin the rest of my life. He took enough from me and I won't let him take still more."

"He's dead and gone, Ivariel," Ochieng murmured, as if in comfort. "He can't ever hurt you again."

I laughed, a dry bitter sound. "But don't you see? He can and does. Every time I think about..." I had to swallow, my throat tight and resisting. "About...giving myself that way again...I—"

"Don't weep." He leaned his face toward mine, still not touching me, but it was clear he wanted to. "I'm sorry I forced you to talk about this. You don't have to say any more."

I scrubbed the tears away impatiently, with fury at the way they just fell like that, without my knowledge or control. "I do have to say it. I think you're probably better giving up on me. I don't know that I'll ever be able to submit to that again. I'm not sure I can... make myself. Do you understand?"

I looked into his eyes, seeing that he thought he did, but he didn't. Not really.

"It doesn't have to be like that," he told me. "It can be joyful, a mutual sharing of pleasure. Not submitting or giving yourself, but partaking. Like eating or drinking—it's a way of feeding ourselves."

I understood that. Or, rather, somewhat understood. The rekjabrel and concubines, some of them, had relished bed sport and spoke of it with enthusiasm. My father's wives had loved to be called to his bed, though I mistrusted that, as they mostly wanted the opportunity to influence him. My teachers in the sensual arts, however, had made it clear that the giving of pleasure mirrored the receiving of pleasure. I was far from ignorant in that arena. It made me smile to think that Ochieng saw me as some innocent when I'd learned my sensual skills in the seraglio of the Imperial Palace. Should I choose to—or could find a way to make myself—I could shatter those illusions and likely pleasure him as no other woman in all of Chiyajua could.

"You laugh at me?" he asked, though not offended.

"No. Never that," I answered. "But you still don't understand."

"Tell me then."

"It's not you I don't trust. It's me."

His dark gaze searched my face. "How so?"

"Ochieng, I had no plan to kill Rodolf. I planned to die. No, don't say anything." I'd raised my hand and laid my fingers over his lush mouth before I realized it, surprising us both.

He turned his head ever so slightly, back and forth, brushing the lightest of kisses against my fingertips. I pulled them back, cupping them in the palm of my other hand, as if to save the caress.

"Ever since my wedding night—or, perhaps later, after I emerged from the shock of it all—I began to hate."

"You deserved to," Ochieng replied, hushed. "Anyone would have felt the same."

"Maybe? But I mean that this…I think of it as a kind of dark seed of hatred that found fertile soil in my heart. By the time I realized how I'd nourished it, how deeply it had wound itself through all my soul, I had no idea how to root it out. All I could do was try not to give it more than I already had, because I was afraid it would destroy me. When I went to meet Rodolf, I stopped worrying about it destroying me. I fed it with everything in me."

"So it would destroy him." Ochieng kept his face calm, but a deep anger showed in his eyes.

"I don't know if I thought that clearly. I just stopped caring what happened to me. I only knew I'd never let them take me back to Dasnaria. I wanted to die here, on the soil of Chiyajua."

"Oh, Ivariel." His face creased into a kind of grief. "I don't know what to say."

"It's a good thing. You offered me this place, said it was my home, and I wanted—still want—that. And if I had to die, it would be here. I gave myself over to that. It wasn't until he…" I took a ragged breath. Behind me Efe shifted, leaning her shoulder into me. "When he asserted his marital rights, that's when I lost control of the serpent."

"I'm glad," he breathed. "He deserved to die."

"I think so, too," I agreed. "And I don't regret killing him, or any of those men who died that night, and that's maybe a problem. I don't feel anything for their deaths, except perhaps a kind of satisfaction."

"I understand."

"Do you?" My turn to search his face. He certainly wanted to understand, but I didn't think wanting would be enough. "I'm glad I killed him." Interesting how it felt to say as much aloud. "I'm glad he's dead instead of me. But that's not my point. Ochieng, I don't remember killing him. I don't have much memory of that night at all. Not really. It's like a dream I remember having long ago."

"Some things we don't remember in order to protect ourselves, because it hurts us too much. As you heal and grow stronger, you'll recall more and be able to make sense of what happened."

I smiled and felt terribly old. I loved Ochieng's optimism, his brightness of spirit. He couldn't understand the dark paths I'd gone down. "I don't think that's it. It seems that this serpent lives its own life now, borrowing my body. I may be Ivariel on the skin, but I think Jenna became a monster. She's in me and she's stronger than I am. She has all the strength of her hatred."

"So, you learn. You will heal and let the hatred go."

"Or I won't, and I'll be as scarred and as untrainable as Efe. She and I, neither of us able to earn our keep, to be a real part of things." As if she understood, Efe blew out a long breath, her trunk questing along my feet, then wrapping around one ankle.

"This is an excellent analogy," Ochieng said. "Don't laugh—it is! Efe suffered, yes, but she's come a long way since her rescue. She's learned a great deal and continues to learn. You never saw her back then, so you can't recognize how far she's come."

I made a sound of dismissal for his idealism and he frowned. "I have no intention of giving up on either one of you, so you can forget that. And you don't have to earn a place here. This is your place. Apparently I haven't made it clear enough to you, but I am in love with you, Ivariel, and I want you to be my wife."

My breath stuck somewhere behind my stomach, making it turn over. I'd forgotten sometime in the winding of this confessional that I'd suspected him to be on the verge of such a declaration. And now I would have to put an end to his hopes.

"That can't ever be," I told him, making it sound as final and as irrevocable as possible.

"I'd believe that if you hadn't given up the vow of chastity—and if you'd asked for the disk back when I offered it."

He had a point there. As difficult as I found it to explain, I figured I owed him that. "The reason I don't think I can take up the vow again is that I already broke it with Rodolf."

"That was rape. Danu could hardly hold you accountable for that."

I shook my head. "He was legally my husband. I complied with his orders."

"So would anyone with a knife to her throat."

"He held no knife to my throat." He hadn't had to.

"Because he didn't have to. You were already in his power, he could've killed you or had you killed at any moment, yes?"

"Well, yes, but—"

"I don't wish to interrupt your words, but there are no 'buts' to that. That's a metaphorical knife to the throat. Add to that the fact that you were diligently taught all your life to submit to your husband—to anything any man asked of you, in fact. Isn't that what you told me?"

"Yes." I kind of wished I hadn't told him as much as I had. In that first waking, so grateful to be alive and to see the rains, to be held by him—and in the grip of the pain-lulling tea Zalaika had given me—I'd revealed so much of my life, myself to him. My teeth ached from clenching my jaw. "None of this is the point."

"Then what is the point?" He asked it gently, encouragingly, but with a certain bewilderment.

"The point is that I *didn't* submit! Don't you see? I *killed* him. And I don't remember doing it." Just the blood, so much blood. Painting my bare breasts with it and wishing that he hadn't died so quickly. "I can't trust myself," I told him, in a ragged whisper. "I don't know when it will happen again, what will set me off... who I might kill next. It could be anyone—even you."

~ 3 ~

Ochieng studied me, his confusion clearing. "This is why you won't carry your blades, why you won't take up your dances and martial practices."

"All you need is for me to lose my mind again like that with a blade in my hand."

"It's different. You're not in peril from me."

"Remember when you kissed me that first time?"

He smiled with nostalgic delight. "For the rest of my life I'll remember that moment."

"Clearly you don't remember the part where I panicked and hit you!"

"Barely."

"I drew blood."

"It didn't even hurt. I understood then and understand now. Besides, you didn't hit me when I kissed you the second time. Progress."

I looked away from him. The feeling of being trapped rose to a worrying level, the seeds of another panic in it. "Let me go."

Though he hadn't been restraining me, he immediately stepped back, giving me room to move. There wasn't much space to go anywhere, with the elephants crowded under the shelter, the hay-strewn ground prickly under my bare feet. They were caked in mud, which suddenly bothered me greatly. I scraped one foot against the other, accomplishing nothing.

"Feet of clay," Ochieng said. He'd picked up a cloth and sponged the dirt from around Efe's eyes. She liked to bury herself in mud and it accumulated around her eyes, making it hard for her to see. If I'd been a good caretaker, I would've done that for her. Exhaustion slammed through me, so I sat on a stone bench, waiting for him to say more.

He didn't.

"What does that mean?" I finally asked.

Glancing at me, he frowned a little to see me sitting, but didn't comment. "It's a way of saying we're all human and we have flaws. You don't like the mud on your feet, but you couldn't walk out here without getting muddy. You're not an angelic being who can float through the air, untouched by the muck of the world."

"I never claimed to be," I retorted.

Ochieng laughed, surprising me, and came to sit beside me, though a careful distance away. "You know," he said confidingly, "I always thought that poise of yours came from being a Warrior and Priestess of Danu. Now that I understand you're the daughter of an emperor, I wonder how I missed your air of regal command."

I gave him a long look, which only made him laugh again. "Ivariel, my love, I'm only saying that I don't mind the mud. See?" He lifted his own foot, also bare, also caked with mud. "We are all human. And the dirt washes away again."

Usually his sunny attitudes and philosophies amused me. This time, however, with the anger already riding me, the dark frustration at being asked to explain and then him brushing it off... I stood. "I'm going back."

"All right." He stood also.

"Alone," I clarified.

He put a hand on my arm, stopping me, not flinching when I glared at him with all the imperious poise in me. "You can give me your daughter-of-an-emperor stare-down all you like," he said without rancor, "but I've been dealing with powerful females my entire life. If I can handle Violet, I can handle you."

I contemplated the several layers of meaning there. The elephants never frightened Ochieng, even though they could easily crush him in their might and occasional furies—or panics. He waited me out, calm as ever.

"Mull that over," he finally said. "In the meantime, I'm not letting you climb all those stairs alone, because you're weaving on your feet right now. You don't have to marry me. You don't even have to let me help you, but I won't let you endanger yourself."

Something in me broke, and the anger drained away, leaving only the weariness behind. Surprising myself, I leaned against him, finding there the same warmth and strength as in the elephants. I'd surprised him, too, but after a moment his arms came around me, and he held me with infinite tenderness I didn't deserve.

"I'm so tired," I admitted, pressing my face into his wet shirt.

"Then rest," he murmured, cupping my head and smoothing his fingers through my hair. "The rainy season is for resting, not for going out in the mud."

"I feel like I'll never be dry again."

He laughed a little. "So say we all. But the rains always end, and in the hot and dry of summer you'll dream fondly of the cooling rains and think that maybe you'll never see a cloud again."

"Is that another philosophical lesson?"

"Not a lesson—an observation. With time, things change. But you can't force them to your schedule."

"I didn't think I was doing that."

"I think…" He hesitated. "You're tired. We can talk about it later."

"No." I pulled back, looking into his face, but didn't pull away. "You might as well give me all your truth at once." And despite my brave intentions, I wasn't quite ready to face the climb.

He smiled, brushing my hair off my forehead, where a few strands had hung into my eyes. "Your hair is growing longer, and more white now than black."

"I should cut the black off. It probably looks odd," I replied, pulling a strand around so I could see it. Which wasn't much, as my hair was longer than it had been, but not that long. After Rodolf, I'd decided to stop dying it. Well, some of that had been because I'd been asleep or weak as a kitten for so long. By the time I could get up and do the job, it had seemed pointless.

"I like it, the half and half." Ochieng's gaze wandered over my face and hair. "Though it will be interesting to see you with all of your own hair."

"The real me," I pointed out, feeling more than a little grim about it, "emerging no matter what I do."

"The way of the world," he agreed.

"Tell me what you were going to say. You think what?"

He sighed a little, mouth curving in a rueful smile that he hadn't distracted me. "I don't know what it's like to grow up as you did, expecting to rule all around you, but I imagine it gives you certain habits of thinking."

No more princess! I heard Kaja telling me. How I missed her. "You're saying I expect everything to fall into place as I order it?"

Ochieng regarded me gravely. "I wouldn't have put it that way, but… perhaps so."

I nodded, aware of the weakness in my legs. "I'll think on all of this."

"Tomorrow is soon enough. Or the day after that. Or the day after that. Will you let me carry you back up?"

It sounded so good. Such a relief as I wasn't sure I could make it on my own. My pride would be wounded far worse by falling or failing than by having him carry me. "Do you think you can?" I asked.

His face cracked into a wide smile, the sun banishing the rains. "Oh yes. I carried you before. And you weigh less now than then. A bird weighs more."

"I'm trying to eat," I grumbled. He sounded just like his mother, badgering me about putting on some weight. And it hadn't occurred to me that someone would have had to carry me back to the D'tiembo house, up all the stairs, and into bed. I didn't know how I felt that it had been him.

"I know," he soothed, and for a moment I thought he meant about him carrying me before. "Ready? Is there anywhere I need to be careful not to touch you?"

"Well, if I turn into a wild thing and try to kill you, not that spot."

He laughed, throwing his head back. "Ah, good. A joke is a very good sign. You don't frighten me, Ivariel. I'm not so easy to kill as that. Put your arms around my neck."

I did, more aware this time of the shock of bodily contact. He crouched a little, sliding one arm under my knees and the other behind my back, lifting me easily. It made me remember another time, so I shared that thought aloud, rather than keeping it to myself. Another sort of practicing, starting out with easy steps.

"Harlan carried me like this once," I told him.

"Your brother, yes?"

"Yes, my baby brother. On my wedding journey, I rode in the carriage and smoked opos, to kill the pain in my body and the fear in my heart." I waited while Ochieng sprinted across the open area, ducking my head against him and the worst of the downpour. "One day he rode with me— which wasn't easy for him, because he had to pretend to be cold, so the men all teased him for being weak—and he made me stop taking the opos smoke, which numbs pain and all the unpleasantness of the world. He told me that he was going to help me escape, and when we arrived where we were to spend the night, I pretended to be weak and fainting, so he had to carry me. That way he could see the interior of the seraglio, so he'd know how to break me out."

"A clever plan," Ochieng replied, swishing his feet in the tub of water kept there to prevent everyone from tracking in the worst of the mud. Then he began climbing the steps with enviable vigor and speed. "Brave of you to dissemble so."

"Well, it didn't take much on my part. I'd lost a lot of blood and hadn't been eating well then either."

"How long ago was this—can you count it?" Ochieng was aware that I'd only recently learned to count. I'd gotten better at it, but I still had to plod my way mentally through the numbers that came so easily to others.

"Let me think. Ten days after my wedding, which was on my birthday." I stacked up the tens in my mind. "I don't know exactly because I haven't counted every day. But I've had my menses four times since then."

He was quiet a time. "Not even half a full-turn of the seasons then. A short time to expect yourself to have recovered from so much."

"I *am* an Imperial Princess," I informed him loftily. "We have high expectations as a rule."

He laughed, and pressed a fleeting kiss to my temple. "Then I shall have to do my best to live up to that."

"I didn't mean it that way," I protested, stricken.

"A joke only," he assured me. "So far as I've been able to ascertain, your high expectations seem to focus entirely on yourself. You could do with expecting more of the people who claim to be your family."

Ouch—that stung a surprising amount. Though of all the family I'd been born into, only Harlan had tried to help me. And he'd given up everything to do that. Before I killed him, Rodolf had told me that Harlan had taken refuge in the Skablykrr, a sort of philosophical training that allowed him to make binding vows no one could attempt to break. Funny how we'd both resorted to oaths of silence to escape the family fist.

"What happened—is she hurt?" Zalaika interposed herself in our path the moment Ochieng set foot on the house level. She scrutinized me, holding out her hands as if she might pluck me from Ochieng's arms.

"I'm fine," I told her, in their language. Zalaika sometimes forgot how much I'd absorbed—and still hadn't quite gotten in the habit of expecting me to reply. All the D'tiembos did that, habitually turning to Ochieng to translate for me as he'd always been unerringly good at reading into my unvoiced communications. Part of what made him so good at working with the elephants, who thought a great deal, but said nothing. "Just weary today."

"She's fine, Mother," Ochieng chimed in, sounding both cheerful and exasperated. "Can't a man cuddle his woman without an interrogation?" He stepped neatly around his mother and carried me to a chair under an overhang. Rain fell off the grass sheaves in a torrent in that spot, carried away in a trough carved into the rock. "Put your feet under the fall," he told me.

I extended my feet under the water, bemused enough by his kneeling to carefully wash my feet not to protest him calling me his woman. Apparently he'd decided to stake his claim. The wording wasn't as legally definitive as it would be in Dasnarian, but was certainly possessive enough to have Zalaika looking terribly pleased. Better than the alternative, of resenting her eldest son's interest in a damaged foreign woman. From comments she and Ochieng's siblings had dropped, they had expected him to settle on a spouse for quite some time. The clan didn't lack for next generations—in fact, I'd discovered that Ayela and Femi were the grandchildren of Ochieng's older sister, Palesa. But they all seemed concerned that Ochieng hadn't found anyone to marry—Zalaika particularly so.

Perhaps all mothers work to marry off their children.

Zalaika beamed at me and handed me a towel to dry my hair. "You will learn to stay out of the rain," she admonished me. "The elephants have thick skin, not thin and pale like yours. I'll make you a bone broth with plenty of duck fat. That will bring color to your cheeks." She hastened off, singing one of her cooking songs.

I groaned and Ochieng raised a brow at me, taking the towel to dry my now clean feet. "I'm going to turn into bone broth and duck fat," I explained.

He laughed, standing and offering me a hand. "My mother's cure for all things. Welcome to being a D'tiembo."

"Ochieng..." I hesitated, and he watched me expectantly, not helping. "I haven't agreed to anything," I said. In fact, I thought I'd explicitly *not* agreed.

"I know. And that's all right. I'm a patient man."

"Your patience may yield you nothing."

"I'm aware of that also." He laced his fingers with mine and drew me deeper into the house. "Let's sit by the fire and dry off."

"I'm not sure I believe there's such a thing as being dry," I grumbled.

"Oh, there is. Remember: all things change in time."

I *would* have to harbor tender feelings for an incurable optimist. Perhaps I'd simply been attracted to the furthest kind of person from Rodolf I could find.

Perhaps, too, when I'd rested, I'd try some dance steps.

~ 4 ~

The next morning, instead of visiting the elephants, instead of slipping out of the house and into the rain—which, of course, still fell, as unrelenting as ever—I went to the first room, which Ochieng had said they'd cleared for me to dance in.

I'd had every intention of at least trying some the day before, but with a belly full of bone broth with duck fat, and a bowl full of the rich duck meat as well, I'd fallen asleep in the comfortable chair by the fire. I and the three D'tiembo elders napped the afternoon away in our pillowed chairs, only awakening long enough to be fed dinner before we shuffled stiffly off to our beds.

Perhaps because they'd pried me out of it long enough, my room had been refreshed, with clean—dry!—bedding in place and even my sodden interior curtains swapped out for dry ones. Not that they stayed that way for long, but that and the warm brazier that greeted me made for a good, long sleep. I didn't know how much one person could sleep. If Ochieng counted my numbers correctly, it had been half a year since I turned eighteen. I must have spent most of it asleep.

In the morning, however, as if some sort of timer had flipped over, its sands falling the other direction, I truly did feel better. Enough to say so with some enthusiasm when people asked. I ate my breakfast in the interior kitchen—grain with bone broth and duck fat—listening to the conversations, as I hadn't done since before I got hurt.

"The river is up another knot," Ochieng's brother Desta informed everyone, walking to the fire to dry. As most of them did, he'd shed his wet clothes in one of the outer rooms, then wrapped himself in a loose robe to come deeper inside. The way the house was constructed, with square

rooms formed by four wooden poles, built on top of, beside and below
its neighbor, the more interior the space, the drier it remained, due to the
buffering of the others. Some of the D'tiembos simply left wet clothes
hanging up in one or two of the exterior rooms to wear out into the rain. I
hated putting on damp clothes, but that was apparently just me.

"The next flight of steps?" Ochieng asked.

Desta swept his hand across. "Gone entirely. That's four flights this
season."

"The river will take what's hers," Zalaika sang out, as if vastly amused.
"That will teach you to predict short rains. I hope you've learned some
humility."

Desta gave her the same fondly exasperated look Ochieng often had in
dealing with their mother. "Yes, well, if the rains don't end soon and we
reach two more marks, we'll have to move the stores from the first level."

"If the rains don't end soon," Ochieng's sister Palesa replied, "we'll
have to pull out of the top level rooms. We're starting to get leaks. The
grass sheaves are saturated."

Desta threw up his hands. "That amount of work should inspire enough
exhausted humility to satisfy even you, Mother."

"Ah, and the river? We shall see what satisfies *her*."

"What about the elephants?" I asked, startling everyone, heads swiveling
to look at me. They still forgot I possessed a voice.

"We won't forget them, Ivariel." Ochieng smiled at me from across the
way. "They will always be first priority with the D'tiembos."

"Fortunately," Desta added, "the elephants can move themselves and
require no heavy lifting."

I blushed a little at the teasing. "I didn't mean to imply you would
forget them."

"Your concern does you credit, Priestess." Zalaika came to take my
bowl away, patting my shoulder in approval that I'd eaten it all. "You may
not be born of D'tiembo, but you have the heart of one, always thinking
first of our elephant kin."

Desta made a snorting sound, but Ochieng's two sisters sitting nearby,
weaving cloth, sent up a chiming song of happy agreement, one that I'd
decided translated roughly as "we love our elephant kin," if a Dasnarian
were ever to say something so bizarre. Ochieng still smiled at me, but it
deepened somehow, in a warmly intimate way, and I had to avert my gaze.

"We should begin moving stores to the higher levels now," Desta returned
to his point. "No sense waiting."

"If we pack things too tightly, we'll get mold," Palesa replied. "And rot."

"Rain means mold and rot," Desta retorted. "There's no avoiding it entirely."

"There's avoiding it mostly," the other sister Thanda put in, never looking up from the thread she spun. "And that means not packing things in more tightly than we absolutely have to."

They fell into an intense debate on the topic and I made sure not to insert my opinion. Instead, I left them to the arguing—which they seemed to enjoy as much as storytelling—and went to the first room.

The first room, as implied by the name, was the first built by Ochieng's ancestor when he first settled in Nyambura. Removing his beloved elephants from danger, and changing his name to D'tiembo, he'd come to this great rock outcropping at the curve of the river and established a safe home for all of them. He built the first room, which was the entirety of the home he shared with his wife and first child for many years.

As the family grew, so did the house, one room adding onto the next. Because it sat at the center and bottom, the first room felt cave-like in its darkness, the floor the simple granite foundation, polished smooth over the generations of feet. The rooms on three sides were used for storage, and the fourth served as a connector to a much bigger room, where we'd eaten breakfast and the family tended to gather during the rains.

Nobody much liked to use first room, because it was smaller and darker than the others, but they also felt disrespectful using it for storage. So they kept it clean and tidy, with a few treasured family mementos displayed, and pillows for reclining on. These last Ochieng had moved—or more likely, had the children move—to the back corners, leaving a clear space in the middle. It made for a smaller space than I'd danced in back in the seraglio, but substantially larger than my cabin on the first ship I'd sailed on, the *Valeria*, when I'd danced in the dark by myself, to keep from losing my mind entirely.

I liked first room for its coziness and sense of history. Pausing a moment, I admired one of the four wooden posts that served as the foundation for so much. Bigger around than three of Ochieng, they must have come from truly great trees—which could only be found in the forest a few hours' journey by elephant from the town of Nyambura that had grown up around the house. D'tiembo used his elephants to harvest the trees and float them down the river, to be caught in the weir he'd built across it for the purpose.

A clever man, D'tiembo. I always pictured him in my mind as Ochieng, which I knew wasn't accurate, but the image stuck that way, perhaps because it was Ochieng who had told me the stories. His voice carried from the other room, jovially talking over Desta, saying something about patience.

I ran my fingers over the simple patterns carved into the wood, dark with age. Chains of elephants followed each other in spirals. Flowers bloomed between them, birds darting in and out, carrying garlands. All four posts had the same elephant parade, but three differed in the other elements. One had fish and reeds, another ducks and lily pads, the last lionesses and the mushroom-looking trees of the grass plains. I went from one to the next observing the similarities and differences, as I hadn't before.

"For each of their children," Zalaika said, coming into the area and joining me at the post with the lionesses. She tapped one. "This was their first daughter, Zema, named for the lion queens who roam the plains. They are astonishing to see."

"I saw some," I told her. "On the journey here."

"Did you?" She gave me a thoughtful look. "Ochieng didn't tell me this."

Because I hadn't told him. I couldn't have, at the time, with my vow of silence intact, but I might not have anyway. The dawn vision of the three lionesses had felt … sacred in a way. I wasn't at all sure what moved me to tell Zalaika now. Something about the carvings on the pole reminded me of those lions and the way their eyes had glowed as they took my measure.

"Only I saw them," I told her. "Just before the sun rose. Three of them. They appeared out of the mist, looked at me, and left again."

Zalaika hummed in her throat. "A powerful vision."

That hadn't occurred to me. "I think they were real."

She laughed, husky and not unkindly, patting me on the arm. "I'm sure they were. I simply mean that they came to give you an important message, appearing only to you, at that time."

"What message?" I asked.

"Only you can know that, as it was for you. Three powerful females, sisters, maybe. Perhaps that will mean something to you, if it doesn't already."

Sisters. The thought hit me with startling clarity. Could it be about my sisters and me? Inga and Helva had promised to be there when I returned to Dasnaria. I'd at least managed to spare them my fate, but unless they chose to marry—and they would not be forced to, if the emperor and my mother kept their promises—they would live out their lives in the seraglio of the Imperial Palace. Golden blond and lethal in their graceful ways, they could be my sister lionesses.

What did that mean, though? We would never be together again. I couldn't return to Dasnaria, and they would never be allowed to leave.

"We've all adopted this tradition," Zalaika said, running her fingers over the carvings as I had. "When we marry, the couple chooses a set of four posts to make a new room, and they carve it with designs. If children come, the parents add images to represent each child and what we name them."

"What images did you carve for Ochieng?" I asked, suddenly curious.

"The sun, of course," she replied. Then cocked her head at my expression. "His name means 'of the sun.'"

Of course it did. A shiver ran over me, that sense of Danu's hand.

"You will have to come see our poles sometime," Zalaika continued. "They become part of the history of this house, see? The foundation of the home and also of the family."

I carefully didn't meet her expectant gaze. Though I remembered how Ochieng had asked me that about the tree we'd harvested together. He'd said it would make four excellent poles if I'd like to help carve them. I'd nodded agreement and he'd been so happy. With a stab of sheer alarm, I realized that had been his version of an offer of marriage. Zalaika's gaze weighed on me, making me wonder if Ochieng had told her *that*.

It shouldn't count. Right after that everything had gone to chaos, with the news of Kaja's death and my late husband's imminent arrival. Besides, I hadn't known what Ochieng was truly asking, or I wouldn't have agreed. Even if I'd wanted to agree, I couldn't have as Dasnarian women can't make those kinds of legal decisions.

Though…I wasn't Dasnarian anymore. I'd made myself into a widow through my own actions, why not make my own self into a wife? Despite Ochieng's confident assurances that he could handle me should I descend into madness, I had no such faith. I couldn't possibly have children, not knowing what uncontrollable violence lay buried in the fetid detritus of my soul.

"I think I'll try dancing a bit," I told her, hoping she'd go away, but Zalaika nodded and surveyed the room, making sure all was ready.

"How do you dance without music?" she asked. "I've long wanted to ask you this. It seems impossible to me."

I had to laugh. Zalaika—indeed, all the people of Chiyajua it seemed—conducted every aspect of their lives to music. They sang along with the *negombe* that pulled the caravan wagons. They sang dinner chants, cleaning chants, elephant chants. The sisters even continued to hum their weaving music under the conversation, interrupting themselves to argue about mold and the river, then picking up the tune again.

"When I learned, I had music," I told her. "The women sang and chanted the dance songs."

"No instruments?"

"Where I grew up, I lived entirely with women, and women did not play instruments, so no."

Zalaika looked aghast and avidly curious. I should have anticipated that more than Ochieng would have questions about my past—and had answers ready. I didn't care to expose my family and culture to their judgment more than necessary. Struggling to see what I came from more objectively would be enough challenge without feeling I needed to somehow defend it. But I did know something about directing conversation.

"It is a wonderful tradition among *my* family," I told her, "that we sing the songs and pass along the dances from mother to daughter. The music lives in our hearts and needs no other instrument."

Zalaika considered that, pursing her lips. A gleam of understanding in her dark eyes, so like her son's, indicated that she might see through my gambit, but she also allowed it. "Perhaps you'll teach us *your* song then? We shall sing for your dance. Palesa and Thanda! Come in here. Ivariel is going to teach us one of her people's songs." She smiled at me with such artless pleasure that I might've believed she hadn't neatly taken control of the conversation again.

Palesa and Thanda came in, carrying pieces of their weaving, wearing excited smiles, and settled themselves on pillows. Ochieng followed, leaning a shoulder against one post and giving me a questioning look. If I asked him—even by the slightest gesture—he would save me from his mother and sisters.

As soon as I thought it, the absurdity of my trepidation hit me. These women only longed for diversion. A new song, a dance, to relieve the boredom of the rains. And to get to know me better. They posed no threat to me. Rather the reverse.

Thinking of the lionesses I'd seen, and of my sisters, I began singing a simple song, one for little girls first learning to dance. Not the ducerse, the demanding dance I'd shown my students, the one Kaja had deemed the most adaptable to martial use. We called this one the Silly Snail. Being a children's song, it had simple, repetitive words, an easy tune.

As I chanted the first lines, Zalaika and the others—even Ochieng, to my surprise—singing them back, I caught sight of Ayela peeking from the next room, so I beckoned to her. She came running with a wide smile of delight, taking the hand I offered her and following along with my steps.

My body protested, those deep muscles not liking the undulating movements of even that easy dance, but it also felt good to move, to not feel so fragile and tentative. More children joined us dancing, and more adults in the singing, until it seemed all the D'tiembos not in the storehouse had pressed in around the first room. They even shifted some stores from the neighboring rooms, tying back the curtains to make more space.

As the people of Chiyajua loved to do, the adults began embroidering on the refrains, adding in words from their own language. So odd to hear the Dasnarian song of my childhood mixed with Nyamburan words and sung in men's voices, too, their clapping and stomping a masculine underscore to the higher women's melodies.

They were having so much fun—and so was I, amazingly enough—that, though my body ached like an overstretched length of old leather, and I poured with sweat, I taught them another song and dance, and then another.

Until Ochieng whispered in Zalaika's ear and she called a halt for lunch. After which I slept the afternoon away again. Only later, after dinner, did I realize I hadn't gone to see the elephants. Anticipating me, Ochieng told me he'd gone while I slept. They were fine and Efe sent her best wishes for a full recovery. Violet said to send more melons.

The voices he used for the elephants' messages made me laugh.

It had been a good day.

"Yes," Ochieng replied, and I realized I'd said it aloud. "And every day can be just as good, like this."

~ 5 ~

I stood in the driving rain, drenched to the bone, trying to coax a stubbornly terrified Efe out of the elephant shelter.

Even though she stood in swirling water up to her knees, the young elephant swung her head ponderously back and forth like ancient Mara back in the seraglio. I could almost hear her querulously refusing tea, afraid it might be poisoned. Of course, in the seraglio, that had been a real fear. Efe was like me—afraid of what she didn't know.

"Efe, darling, come *on*." I had my arms tangled in her trunk, not exactly pulling on it—try pulling an elephant by the trunk and see what happens—but kind of hugging and tugging at once. She backed deeper into the now empty shelter, dragging me with her. I lost my footing, as knee-deep water for her meant thigh-deep for me, and she kept me upright by pulling me against her, nudging me into the fold of her leg and chest, as if we'd be safe that way.

"We're going to have to get stern with her," Ochieng shouted over the pounding of the rain. "All the others are on high ground. There's no time left for coaxing."

The river had reached Desta's two more marks and higher. Everyone—except me—had been working the last three days to move the goods in the storehouse to the second level. An enormous storm upstream decided the matter. Debate became moot as the river rose so fast that it surged just below the first level almost overnight.

I wasn't allowed to lift anything, even the children running up to take things from me if I tried, but Ochieng gave in when I pointed out that I could at least help with the elephants. Or rather, he succumbed in the face of my imperiously informing him I'd do as I liked, so he might as well go along if he wanted to ensure my safety and good health.

He'd laughed and held up his hands in resignation, muttering to himself about his poor choices in love. I pretended not to hear. The whole exchange left me warm with an odd burst of affection. It made no sense that I'd be at my happiest in the midst of this crisis. But then I'd been miserable surrounded by luxury.

It seemed happiness came from something other than easy circumstances.

The D'tiembos had a system for dealing with the flood waters, and I wore a long rope tied around my waist, anchoring me to the solid storehouse across the way. And I'd grown stronger, too, in the last weeks, practicing my dances while the rains fell without pause, regaining my leg muscles and wind. Though I still left my sword and knives closed in a chest in my room.

"You can't hurt her," I yelled back at him, which wasn't fair, because Ochieng would never willingly hurt an elephant.

Lighting cracked overhead and Efe jumped, rearing a little and backing against the rock face. Ochieng cursed and put his arms around me, speaking rapidly to Efe in the patois he used just with the elephants.

"If it comes to that," he said in my ear when Efe stopped trying to stomp us, "if we have a choice between binding her and forcing her to come or abandoning her to the floodwaters, which do you choose?"

It made me unreasonably angry that he posed it as my choice. They were his elephants, weren't they? "She's too big to float away," I said, stubborn as Efe. Her eye, so near mine, rolled with fear.

"Not if she gives up."

"No manacles," I replied after a moment. "Not ever again. We promised her." The elephant's ankles bore the ridged white scars of the manacles she'd worn for her captors. Ochieng's gaze went to my own wrists, and the similar scars I bore, resignation in his eyes.

"We don't even have manacles," he answered. "I meant ropes."

"Absolutely not." Efe and I, both completely unreasonable.

"What will move her then?" He asked me, as if I'd know. But perhaps I did, if I knew Efe's heart like my own.

"Who," I replied. "Someone she trusts. We need Violet."

He only paused a moment. "Do you want to get her or shall I?"

All the other elephants had gone up the long path to the mesa that the D'tiembo granite butte thrust out of. I suppose Ochieng gave credit to my greatly recovered strength by even asking the question, though I suppose both jobs would be equally difficult—climbing the steep path or calming Efe.

Lightning cracked again, followed by sonorous thunder. A bad omen. Efe moaned along with it, doing her best to squinch her great self into a ball. The first day I met the elephants, Ochieng had called them mice in huge bodies. If Efe lost her mind, I'd never be able to stop her from flinging herself into the raging waters.

"I'll go," I told him.

He gave me a long very serious look, grabbing my hand and holding it tightly. "Do I have to remind you to be very, very careful?"

I glanced at the new river of water, where there had been the ankle deep mud only weeks before. I never thought I'd miss that mud. "I'm climbing out of the water and going uphill. You're the one staying here with a crazy and dangerous female." I petted Efe in apology with my free hand, though she hardly noticed. "I should warn you to be very, very careful."

"I happen to like crazy and dangerous females." He gave me a crooked grin.

On impulse, I wrapped my fist in his shirt and kissed him. The first time since that morning I woke up. And not a gentle kiss as it had been that day. I opened my mouth and kissed him with all the skill I'd never used for that, stroking the tender inside of his lips with my tongue. He made a sound, let go my hand, and snagged me around the waist, pulling me tight against him as he returned the kiss in kind, his mouth as clever as the rest of him. The world faded into background, the water swirling around my thighs an echo of the surging inside me.

Hot, dizzying, exhilarating, I fell into the pleasure of the kiss. This, it seemed, I could have with Ochieng, unsullied by memories of the past.

"We're working ourselves to exhaustion and you two are kissing in the elephant shed?" Hart yelled over the rain, and we sprang apart, guilty as charged. Hart had traveled with us on the ship from Ehas and familiarity made him easy with teasing us.

"Calming the elephant," Ochieng called back with an unrepentant grin. "Cuddling always makes them more relaxed."

Oddly enough, Efe did seem less wild.

"I'll remind you of that story later." Hart shook his head. "Desta sent me to tell you everything is moved and the river looks to be surging. We're to get back to the house."

"Not yet," Ochieng and I said together, exchanging bemused looks.

"We have to move Efe," he said.

"I have to get Violet," I said.

Hart looked between us. "You both are crazy."

"Go with Ivariel up the butte," Ochieng told him. "She can use your help."

WARRIOR OF THE WORLD

Hart gave him an astonished—and somewhat panicked look. "With what? I can't ride the elephants."

"You can make sure she doesn't drown," Ochieng snapped back, uncharacteristically terse and commanding.

"It's all right," I told Ochieng.

"Hart is going with you," he replied, staring down the young man. "He owes both of us."

Hart threw up his hands. "Fine, fine. At least it's uphill."

"I'll be back as fast as I can," I told Ochieng, wishing I could kiss him again. Suddenly I felt as if I'd wasted enormous amounts of time, not kissing him all this while.

"You take all the time you need to be safe," he returned, dark gaze going to my mouth, making me think he wished the same. He patted Efe. "We'll be fine."

The elephant reached a questing trunk to me, and I let her snuffle the sensitive thumb-like tips around my fingers, a sort of elephant kiss. I unknotted the rope from around my waist, retied it to a post of the overhang, and joined the impatient Hart. Without looking back—which would only make me want to stay—I waded with him out the uphill side of the pavilion. There a broad path led from the elephants' usual grounds, winding up the butte.

I'd gone that way before, that day Ochieng took me to see the forest on the other side of the ridge. But the resemblance between that hot and dusty road and this had long faded into a dreamlike past. Hart and I waded out of the deeper torrent fairly quickly, to my relief, but the steep path was hardly easier to navigate. A stream ran down the middle, carving a steep gully filled with rushing water. In addition, the rain had stripped away the looser dirt and gravel, leaving larger—and sharper—rocks behind. Pride wouldn't let me fail in front of him. It helped, too, in the most difficult sections, for one person to anchor themself and help the other up.

I had no idea how Violet would manage, but I was thinking one step at a time.

Another good reason to have Hart along—he knew the direction to the upper elephant pasture. I hadn't been there before, but he had, helping cut hay before the rains. It looked like a small lake rather than a meadow, but there were the elephants, stoically weathering the downpour, snaking up bundles of drowned grass with their trunks and munching as if the storm didn't rage around them.

"We're going to be hauling food up here for days," Hart observed mournfully, hardly winded from the climb, unlike me. Together we surveyed the area from the hummock of grassy land we stood on. Soggy, but at least not underwater. "At least. Longer if the rains keep going."

According to the D'tiembo records, the longest rainy season had ended ten days before this one, making our current rains a record breaker, at least within their family history. And the storms kept intensifying, not abating. Lightning like this happened only rarely, and usually early in the season. I hadn't asked how long the food would hold out. The storehouse had seemed so robust and full to me, but even I could see that consolidating four stories into three hadn't made it look any fuller. Elephants ate a *lot* and supplies were dwindling.

"Violet!" I yelled to the big matriarch, waving my hands to catch her attention. No sense plunging into the water if she could come to me.

Hart gave me a funny look. "It's so odd to hear you even talk, and then you yell. What is that accent anyway?"

Violet had heard me and turned in our direction, sloshing through the chest-deep water toward me, so I spared Hart a glance. Odd that he didn't know. But then, he also didn't bunk with the family, instead sharing sleeping barracks with a bunch of the other workers. I'd always been a bit bemused by the difference between my status and his. Hearing Ochieng declare his long-held interest in me explained a great deal.

"Dasnarian," I said.

"Huh." He frowned. "Never heard of it."

"You're not missing anything," I replied, my attention on Violet, then realized what I'd said. How disloyal of me. My marriage had been terrible, but that didn't make all of Dasnaria bad. Many people lived in and loved my homeland. Then Violet reached us and I didn't have to explain—or think about that. We had to get down the hill, and back up again. Oh, and then down again. Wonderful.

I gave Violet the hand signal to kneel, and she lifted her ears in surprise, but blew out a long breath and levered her front end down. Before she finished, I'd leapt onto her upraised knee and climbed, settling myself into the familiar nook behind her ears, and urging her to stand again. From Violet's great height I looked down at Hart, who now seemed forlorn and bedraggled, down on the ground alone.

"Want a ride down?" I called to him.

"Glorianna, no!" He cut his hands in negative emphasis, just in case I misunderstood, apparently. "No way am I risking my life."

"She's gentle as a kitten. You can ride behind me."

"No way," he repeated. "I'm safer walking." And, as if to prove his point, he turned and headed determinedly back down the trail, shoulders hunched against the rain.

Violet turned to look at the lake, and I realized I should mind myself—and my mount. Violet had a mischievous bent that led her to try to dunk her rider in the nearest body of water if they weren't paying attention. With no saddle, reins or other means to direct the big creature, an elephant rider had to hone her intention. I'd gotten somewhat good at it before my injuries, but I hadn't been on her since.

Ochieng would sing to her—to all the elephants, much as the caravan drivers sang to the *negombe*—but I hadn't learned those songs. Besides, before I'd been under my vow of silence and had learned to communicate with Violet silently. Funny that it seemed unfamiliar now.

But I concentrated on the image of Efe and Ochieng, back under the pavilion, waiting for us—and Violet turned her own attention to the path leading down the hill, and swung into motion. To my infinite relief. It hadn't occurred to me until that moment that Violet might detect the monster inside me and refuse to obey.

Of course, it could be that Violet had known that about me all along. Probably better than I did, as I hadn't realized the scope of my monstrosity until I found myself dealing death with unholy glee.

Not something to be thinking about just then. *Think about where you want to go, not where you don't want to be.*

I'd wondered how the heavier creature would make it down that slippery slope, but she handled it like a champ. We passed Hart immediately, who waved as we went by. Violet managed by essentially leaping over the steep spots, dancing with surprisingly nimble feet over the stones, even lowering her haunches in a controlled slide from time to time.

It was harrowing. And exhilarating. Much like that kiss.

Sometimes it seemed as if the most frightening things turned out to be the most exciting, too.

~ 6 ~

Violet and I made it to the bottom and the pavilion in a quarter of the time it had taken Hart and I to climb up. As it was, the water had risen considerably, up to Ochieng's chest and he hailed us with glad relief—as did Efe, who hurled herself at Violet, her matriarch and adoptive mother. Reaching up to grasp my bare foot while the elephants exchanged greetings, Ochieng surveyed me. His touch, even only on my foot, made me feel as if I'd come home.

"Are you all right?"

I nodded. "Hart is walking down. The path is a mess. More waterfall than road. We should hurry."

"Agreed. Let me see if I can coax Efe along. You direct Violet."

Fortunately the lighting and consequent thunder had rolled away, the torrential downpour even backing off into a softer rain for the moment. I urged Violet back up the hill, and—keeping her trunk entwined with Efe's—she obliged. Ochieng waded along on Efe's other side, both holding onto her stable bulk and guiding her to the path, keeping her from balking and running back for the dubious shelter of the pavilion.

Efe's hide twitched and shivered, but she stayed close to Violet. Much of Efe's panic might have come from the other elephants abandoning her as much as from the floodwaters. She could've saved herself a great deal of angst if she'd simply gone with them when they left. The D'tiembos leading the elephants to higher ground had assumed Efe would follow once she saw where they were going. But no, the self-defeating creature had dug in instead, refusing to leave the shelter, to her own sorrow.

Much as I had done when I first fled Dasnaria aboard the *Valeria*, hiding in my dark cabin, too stupid to know I could light a lantern or open the portholes. I'd managed to escape, seeking freedom, but still trapped myself in a new prison of my own fears.

Until Kaja forced the door open and dragged me into daylight. Could I somehow do the same for Efe? I'd had the idea—because Kaja gave it to me—that I might be like her, that I could serve Danu by helping those weaker than myself. Efe possessed size and strength far beyond mine, but fear weakened her. At least the rain didn't frighten me. Other things did though.

Violet started up the hill, nudging Efe along, slightly ahead of her, the younger elephant hustling now and outpacing Ochieng as she left the floodwaters behind. Perhaps I still let fears trap me. I might be cowering in my own dubious shelter, the floodwaters rising while everyone else had moved to safety, waiting for me to join them. I couldn't think about helping Efe until I helped myself.

"Want a ride?" I called down to Ochieng, who scrambled to keep up now. I held a hand down to him, asking Violet to slow, and he grinned at me. Taking a running start, he leapt, grasping my hand and vaulting onto Violet's back behind me.

"Thank you," he said, brushing a kiss against my cheek, then easing back to put a space between us.

I reached back for his hand though, and drew it around my waist. "Sit forward," I instructed, mimicking him as he'd taught me that first day. "In front of her shoulders and under the ears. Grasp with your legs and don't worry about your hands."

He chuckled, sliding both hands around my waist, though lightly, still careful of how he touched me. "Good to know." He was quiet a moment, watching Efe climb the hill, agile as a monkey. "What brought this on?"

I could pretend not to know what he meant, but it occurred to me that facing fears meant speaking about them, too. So I deliberately relaxed, leaning back against his strong chest, aware of how still he held himself. Careful not to startle me.

"I'm tired of being afraid," I told him.

"Ah," he breathed. His hands flexed on my flat belly. With his long arms and my narrow build, he could wrap them all the way around me, perhaps twice. And I worried that I felt too skinny to him, that my hip bones jutted too sharply. I decided that this, too, was part of the being afraid.

"I think I want to try to really work with Efe," I said. "Like I started to before... everything. If you would help."

"I'm happy to help," he replied, not seeming to find it an odd change of subject. Or perhaps he understood how those things connected in my mind. "But I suspect you'll do better without my interference. I've yet to see a clear path into Efe's trust. Perhaps you can show me the way."

Aha. We weren't entirely talking about just Efe then. "If I can find it myself," I told him.

"You will. I believe in you."

Just as Kaja had said to me. I blinked back the tears that pricked my eyes, glad to find I could. Perhaps the days of the tears spilling without my control had passed. "As soon as the rains end, then," I said. "I'll start working with her. *If* they ever end."

"They will." He tightened his arms slightly, a sort of easy embrace. "Everything ends, and the new things begin. You can depend on it."

* * * *

He was right, of course. Even I, who'd never experienced it before, felt the shift in the weather two days later. Despite Desta's dire predictions, the wind changed directions, the clouds began to lighten, then break apart. The rain lessened, then abruptly ceased. The river receded.

And, the sun came out, bright and hot, as if she'd been there all along, trying to burn her way through. Though it was later morning, I went onto the terrace and performed the sunrise prayers to Glorianna. I sang Her song to welcome Her return from night, genuflecting and rising in the ritual Kaja had taught me. My joints and muscles, lax with disuse, protested the strain—but it felt good, too. The burn of effort returned to my body with the sun, fueling and lighting me from within. I'd been sitting idle long enough. With the end of the rainy season, my time of hiding and healing would end also, I resolved.

So, when I finished the prayers to Glorianna, I moved into the ducerse, albeit a deeply modified version. I had a great deal to recover. But I'd never learned any of Danu's forms, so the ducerse was as close as I had. I hummed the music to myself, cupping my palms to the sky, and finally finishing with Danu's salute, the sun near enough to zenith to make the moment perfect.

I held it as long as I could, up on the toes of one foot, my knee bent and upraised, one hand pointed at the sky and the other at my heart. Not anywhere near as long as I used to hold it, but at least I could do it.

And, for the first time, I felt empty handed without my weapons.

Lowering myself, I looked around to find my students with me, following my lead in lowering themselves to flat feet, eyes bright and smiles wide. We were back.

* * * *

The ground dried rapidly, great clouds of steam rising from the saturated soil. I helped with clean up, riding Violet to collect debris, which we dumped in the still raging river. We used a big sled attached to a harness around her chest. It slid over the still-slick mud to the river's edge, where workers like Hart waited to toss the stuff in. I found I loved watching the stuff sweep away, tumbling out of sight in the torrent.

If only I could dispose of my own debris as easily. I'd survived my personal rainy season. I was safe, had a good home, things I loved to do. If I could only clear out all the garbage left behind by the floods that had wracked my soul, I could be free again. I could have clear and fertile fields for planting, like the ones the town people of Nyambura prepared in our wake, as we brought the elephant teams in to clear the detritus. The mud from flooding made the soil even richer, Ochieng said, and the moisture helped the seeds to sprout. Soon enough it would be too hot and dry to grow much besides grass, so the Nyamburans sprang into sowing without delay.

I suspected they all embraced the activity with the same joy I'd found in greeting the sun again. It felt delicious, like a big stretch after a long, nourishing sleep, to be outside doing physical work.

Many tasks needed doing, too. Once the fields had been cleared for planting, Violet and I worked in tandem with Ochieng on Bimyr, the elephants dragging a heavy blade between them to plane the roads flat again. It took many passes and careful direction to keep the blade even and the elephants aligned for the precise angle. Gradually we smoothed out the ruts again, first doing all the ones around the D'tiembo house, then radiating out to handle the ones around town and even the big main road leading into Nyambura from Greater Chiyajua.

Thus, Ochieng and I were among the first to greet the messenger who arrived, riding fast on a mud-splattered horse. I hadn't seen many horses in Chiyajua. The people preferred the slow-moving, steady *negombe* for distance travel. Even I could see, however, that it would still be some weeks before the roads dried enough to bear the heavy traffic of the caravans. As it was, we'd been careful to keep the elephants on the grassy verge of the roads, where the grasses held the soil more solid than the slick mud.

Ochieng offered the man some water from his flask, which the messenger took gratefully, but he refused the offer of hospitality in Nyambura. He passed along a bag of scrolls, if we'd be willing to see them distributed to the correct recipients around the area. I stayed up on Violet's back, keeping her steady and thus Bimyr quiet, too, while Ochieng climbed down to talk with the man, but I could hear most of their conversation—until they moved into a different dialect.

The messenger seemed to be telling a story that had Ochieng looking thoughtful, then concerned. It required much waving of hands on the messenger's part, and enough rapid detail that he seemed relieved to be speaking in his own language. I hadn't really wanted to meet the man, finding I retained quite a bit of shyness around strangers. Not quite a fear, but I was self-conscious of my hard-edged Dasnarian accent and often clumsy pronunciation.

And though I didn't think anyone would come looking for me with my late husband and his men all dead—to be blamed on their late-season journey at the beginning of the worst rainy season on record—I felt better being unremarked on. With my wide-brimmed hat on—a new one that Thanda had found for me when the sun came out, decent enough though too big and I didn't love it as I'd loved the first one Ochieng had given me, that my late husband crushed—my pale hair didn't show. Of course, my fair skin did, but in the Nyamburan clothes I liked to think I didn't stand out so much.

Ochieng had said not to worry, but I did, watching his face crease as the messenger spoke at length. Then he shouldered the bag of scrolls, climbed up Bimyr so she wouldn't have to kneel and disturb the dredge, and smiled over at me. "We can turn back here and make a last pass on the way home. Call it a day. I'm for a hot soak, how about you?"

Palesa and Thanda had cleared out the hot pool the day before and had announced yesterday evening that the natural spring ran clear again. We were all excited to be able to soak again. Ironic, as we'd been nothing but wet for weeks. Still it seemed a different enterprise entirely. I loved the idea of a soak—but I also wouldn't let Ochieng distract me. As soon as we had the elephants turned around and headed back to town, the blade dragging evenly along, I made a point of asking.

"What did that man say? You looked worried."

Ochieng shook his head slightly. "Some disturbing news from downstream. Nothing for you to be concerned about."

"Dasnarians?" I persisted.

He looked surprised, then sent me a reassuring smile. "Oh no! No such thing."

I breathed out a relieved breath. Something about his smile, however, seemed off. Not quite genuine. "Then what?" I asked.

Ochieng looked rueful. "It may be nothing, but word is being spread, as a precaution. The region of Chimto was hard hit by the rains. They sit near the delta of the river and the unusual amount of rain, and the fierce storms that sent so much debris downstream caused a great deal of damage. They lost many buildings, which means they'll need wood. In addition, their fields flooded so badly that much soil washed away, and they have so much standing water that the vegetation is rotting. It will be some time before they are able to plant."

Oh. Well, unfortunate for them, but I didn't understand why that made Ochieng look so grave. "Isn't that good for us?" I asked. "We can trade with them for the wood and food they need."

Ochieng gave me a fond look. "In this you are the optimist. Perhaps it will be as you say."

"But you don't think so."

He gazed into the distance, seeing something I couldn't. "Unfortunately, Chimto is the land of my ancestors, where my great-grandfather grew up."

I began to understand. "The place he left, for its warring ways and greed."

"The very one. The people of Chimto are not much for trading when they run low on goods. Besides which, they resent those of us upstream, who hold no love for them either."

"What are you saying, Ochieng?"

"It could come to nothing. Alarm over a fleeting fear."

I knew, however, the power of fear. "What alarm is the messenger spreading?"

"That we should brace for war."

~ 7 ~

Ochieng wasn't as sanguine as he'd made out to me. We bladed the road on our return, yes, but a somewhat hurried effort. I thought that if he could have easily removed the blade and simply carried it back, he would have. As it was, Ochieng's unspoken agitation affected Bimyr, causing her to get out of step with Violet, which meant the road wasn't as perfectly graded as he normally insisted upon.

A disconcerting sign.

And then Ochieng called over Hart and another man to help me unharness the elephants, while he went off, telling me he'd be right back. I spotted him a bit later, on the second level of the storehouse, talking to Desta. I might not know every dialect of the Chiyajuans, but I could read the alarm in the lines of their bodies. I rather thought he would be a while.

The sun had started to decline behind the ridge, and I was tired and mud-splattered. Now that he'd put the idea in my head, I really wanted that hot bath.

Deciding not to wait for Ochieng, I climbed up the steps to the house. Already I could do it so much better than the day Ochieng had had to carry me back up. Looking back on that day, I seemed so overly dramatic, feeling so sorry for myself. Of course it had taken me time to heal—and it would take more time yet—but I could climb the steps without having to stop and rest. It seemed entirely possible that one day I'd be back to where I'd been before my marriage.

A new start might be within my grasp and the thought made me feel like the optimist Ochieng had named me. Perhaps the damage at Chimto had been exaggerated and the fears of attack would prove groundless.

From my room, I saw the elephants wading into the river, indulging in their clear-weather sunset ritual, Violet and Bimyr hastening to join them. Efe had even gone with them to the river, and she didn't always, so that seemed to be a positive sign. It seemed impossible that such a beautiful, peaceful scene could be disrupted. After all, I'd used myself as a decoy to keep the Dasnarians from coming here and destroying it beneath their armored fists. What could these Chimtoans do?

Someone had left clean clothes for me on my little table, and I nearly whimpered with pleasure. Zalaika, Palesa, Thanda and most of the children had been working nonstop, also, but in washing all the woven cloth that made our clothing and curtain walls. They used collected rainwater in barrels as the river ran too fast still for anyone smaller than an elephant to go in, and then hung the things to dry in the sun.

They'd been working from the inner rooms out, bringing everything that could be moved into the sun to dry thoroughly before it could mold, and I looked forward to having my curtain walls clean and dry again. With my room being on the outer edge of the house, it would no doubt be a while yet. So it made me especially delighted to have clean clothes that smelled of sunshine instead of damp.

To avoid smudging my treasure, I pulled out one of my travelling bags to carry the fresh clothes in, surprised to hear it jingle. Setting the clothes aside, I looked in the bag to see what it might be.

Oh, of course. How astonishing that I hadn't realized immediately. The dull metal of the replacement wedding bracelets my late husband had locked on my wrists when he recaptured me—saying I'd have to beg him for jeweled ones again—shone with a menacing gleam in the slanting light. And attached to the right hand one by its chain still, the obscenely huge diamond he'd returned to my finger.

I'd been unconscious when someone—Ochieng most likely, though I'd never asked—had cut the bracelets off me, then slid off the ring, leaving it dangling by the chain. They'd been waiting for me on a table when I awoke, and one of the first things I'd done when I could get up again was stuff the vile reminders in one of the traveling bags I didn't intend to use again.

It said something about the D'tiembos that such a valuable ring could just sit there while I lay unconscious, and expected to die, and no one took it. Possibly such things had no tradeable worth in Chiyajua, though I doubted that. I'd left it behind when I fled—after having my original, bejeweled bracelets cut off—because I knew the diamond would be too recognizable. An icon of the Arynherk ruling family, the massive marquise diamond always decorated their queen. An irony, in that the diamond remained constant in that scenario, while the women themselves came and went like petals blown by winter winds.

It said something about Rodolf and his arrogance that he'd drag such a precious heirloom halfway across the world just to wrestle it back onto the finger of the young wife who'd hated him enough to make herself into a willing exile from everything she'd known just to escape him. Of course, it had never been about *me*. I could see that much more clearly now. When they married me to him, I'd known that winning the emperor's firstborn daughter represented a political triumph for him and Arynherk.

But I'd been caught up in my mother's careful manipulations, believing the match to be a triumph for me, that I would realize my maternal family's ambitions in the alliance. Not that I'd had any real choice, but I'd embraced the opportunity that marriage represented.

I'd also—in a dazzling display of naivety, in retrospect—believed myself to be wanted. The pearl beyond price. Beautiful, unblemished, perfect in grace and manners. The glint of the cold diamond seemed to mock me for being such a stupid girl. Rodolf had never wanted *me*. I wasn't sure if he'd ever even seen me as a human being. Instead I'd been a doll to him, a trophy to hang jewels on and parade about. No wonder he'd been so cruel to me in his sexual attentions.

He'd said that to me all the time, hadn't he? All the while he'd lashed, cut, tortured, and humiliated me, he'd spoken of his rage against the emperor. Everything he did to me, he'd done as revenge against the man he could never touch.

Feeling ill, I stuffed the diamond and the bracelets back in the bag, shoving them deep into the bottom and knotting the ties to close it, as if to keep them from escaping again. I only wished I could shove down those thoughts and memories as easily. But I couldn't, which was why the rage festered in me—in stupid, betrayed Jenna—leaping out to kill in a senseless fury.

Shaking with reaction, I grabbed up the clothes, no longer caring if I muddied them, and slunk around the edges of the house to take the back steps down to the hot pool. I'd be really happy when they restored the steps down the front of the butte, the ones eaten by the river in her voracious hunger, though I understood those were a lower priority.

Funny—I'd once commanded armies of servants to supply my least whim, except freedom and the ability to chart the course of my own life; now I had all that freedom, endless possibilities with Rodolf dead, and it annoyed me to be inconvenienced. Another way, perhaps, that I was fundamentally lacking. Another deep crack in what should be a smoothly packed road.

Ochieng and Desta, along with a number of the other men, had clustered together, clearly having a serious discussion. They reminded me at that moment of my own brothers, and the other men at my debut parties, talking relentlessly of war, hunting, and other conflicts. It could be that men everywhere shared that fascination.

I can move silently and unobtrusively when I try, so I slipped around the edges of sacks of meal and stacks of hay, all still tightly packed in from being moved to the higher levels. Ochieng was turned away from me—the long queue of shining black hair trailing down his back, a stark river against the white shirt, his strong profile just visible—so he didn't see me pass. Which came as something of a relief, with all the poisonous thoughts running around in my head.

Why did *he* want me? He said he was in love with me, but I had no idea how anyone knew that. Besides, no one marries for love. If it was even a real thing, which I doubted, rather than something for naïve girls to sigh over—and to make the ballads of tragic romances all that much more poignant. Maybe love had been invented as a lure to make young girls like I'd been more pliable. We didn't have a choice over who our fathers and brothers married us to, but it went easier for the family if we jumped in willingly, eyes shining, hoping for some mythical bliss.

Especially a second time, knowing what we did about how handing our bodies over to our husbands would be. What could possibly entice a woman to do that, but for the promise of something like love? Well, and children. Having children might be worth it, if the bed sport could be endured. It might be possible, with a gentle man.

It can be joyful, a mutual sharing of pleasure. Not submitting or giving yourself, but partaking. Like eating or drinking—it's a way of feeding ourselves. Ochieng had said those words with great sincerity, as he did everything, so I knew he believed it, at least.

But if so, he could have that with any woman—and clearly had, the way he spoke about it—so none of this answered the question of what he thought he'd get out of marriage to me. He certainly harbored no ambitions for political power in the Empire of Dasnaria. Despite my dour thoughts, that image very nearly made me smile. He said he found me beautiful, and I suppose my face still was, more or less. Rodolf had called me beautiful, also, and that did not mean he cared about me.

I wished I understood what Ochieng wanted from me. Children, perhaps. That I could believe in—that children brought joy and pleasure, even a kind of love, though a different sort, to a woman's life. I'd observed that.

I didn't know anyone who'd been in love with their husband, did I? Deep in thought, I strolled along the path to the hot pool. Princess Adaladja, who I'd met at my debut ball, had expressed affection for her husband, saying she missed sleeping with him at night, separated as their chambers had been at the Imperial Palace. And there had been the married couple on the *Robin* who'd traveled with us to Chiyajua. They'd seemed to enjoy each other's company at least. But was that love?

In the end, it didn't matter. Love was demonstrably not necessary for marriage, or to produce children. So, I needed to disregard that part of Ochieng's proposal. Whatever he believed, this idea that he loved me had to be subsidiary to his true reasons. I would have to find out what they were.

I would not go blindly into marriage again, naïvely hoping for some joyful state of bliss. I'd been ignorant before, which might not have been entirely my fault, but my eyes had been opened—brutally and painfully— and I would not willingly close them again.

~ 8 ~

Feeling resolved in that determination, if not exactly lighter in spirit, I rounded the spur of rocks to the hot pool. Then skidded to a stop when I found it occupied.

Before I'd come to Nyambura, the custom had been for the D'tiembos to stop on the far side of the rocky outcropping and call out to find if the hot pool was occupied—and whether they were amenable to more company. To accommodate me and my vow of silence, they'd gone to hanging a flag at the rocks, affording me the privacy I preferred. They'd found it odd, but as in all things, they accommodated my foreign quirks.

I realized, too late, that not only hadn't I seen the flag, the pole it had hung on had disappeared. Washed away in the rains, no doubt. And I'd failed to call out, having never been in that habit.

Blushing furiously at my gaffe, I stammered an apology to Zalaika, Palesa, and Thanda. They'd jumped at my unexpected arrival and now laughed, fanning themselves over the start I'd given them.

"I'm so very sorry," I repeated, and hastily turned to go.

"Don't be silly," Palesa called out. "Join us."

"Yes," Thanda added. "It's right you should join us for the first celebratory soak."

I turned back cautiously, trying not to see the three naked women all smiling at me. In the seraglio, of course, being all women—except for the small boys—we'd all gone naked as often as not. But with the D'tiembo matriarchy, seeing them so felt like an invasion. Also, in the seraglio, the emperor's other wives would resent any intrusion on time they spent tutoring their daughters. All of my private meetings with my mother had been zealously guarded, on pain of flogging for anyone who'd dared to interrupt us.

"Please do join us," Zalaika said, and it sounded like a command, despite the polite phrasing. "This is our annual ritual, to savor the fruits of our labors, to be the first in the hot baths."

"And to don the clothes *we* cleaned," Palesa added, Thanda nodding in vehement agreement.

I realized I still clutched the clothes they'd left me and hadn't thanked them. What an ungrateful, unmannered thing they must think me. Silence had been easier. "Thank you so much," I said, bowing a little, "for the clean clothes. I was delighted to find them and in my haste, thought only of getting clean and putting them on. I won't intrude on you."

"You're not intruding, girl." Zalaika sounded impatient now. "I'd tell you if you were. Of course you want to get clean and dry. Get out of those muddy things and get in the water."

"Or we'll drag you in." Palesa grinned in mischief, turning to Thanda. "Remember when we did that to our cousin?"

Thanda burst out laughing, a sound very like Ochieng's. "And she'd just done her hair because she was flirting with that boy. She had a *fit*!"

"Yes," Zalaika said repressively, "and I was the one who had to make it good with her mother. Cost me a length of indigo-dyed cloth to appease her."

"Sorry, Mama," Palesa said, sounding contrite, but her eyes still sparkled with amusement and Thanda unsuccessfully smothered a giggle.

Desperately I tried to think of a polite way to refuse them, but Zalaika had me skewered in place with her dark, knowing gaze. "I'm going to say this plain to you, Ivariel. I know you like your privacy, but I suspect some of that comes from you wanting to hide what was done to you."

Rooted with horror, my insides going to water, I couldn't say anything.

She nodded knowingly. "We've seen your scars—the old and the new, you know."

"We sponge-bathed you and changed your bandages while you were ill," Palesa said more gently than her mother. "We three," she tipped her head at Thanda, who shrugged a little, as if it had been no great effort.

"What Mama is saying so badly," Thanda said, "is you don't have to worry about us seeing you, because I know your skin as well as my babies' at this point. And if you want to get clean anywhere nearly as badly as I did, then you should get in here immediately."

I knew when I'd lost. So, I set my precious clean clothes on a rock ledge next to theirs, and stripped off my muddy things, leaving them in a heap, also with theirs. They'd gone back to chatting, affording me the privacy of not watching me undress, and made room for me as I got in.

Closing my eyes, I tipped my head back on the rim and pretended I was alone. Which lasted about half a minute.

"Dunk your head, Ivariel," Palesa said, "and I'll soap your hair for you. We all already did, and that will give time for the suds to clear."

I'd noticed they all had their hair down and wet, making them look softer than they usually did, with their locks efficiently tied out of the way of their work. Obediently—and unwilling to inconvenience their bath more than I had—I slid under the water, scrubbing my fingers through the short hair to dislodge the worst of the muck.

Palesa was ready with a bar of the soap they made, a spicy strong-smelling variety, nothing like the lavish jasmine-scented soaps and oils I'd grown up with. Even the memory of the smell of jasmine had my already queasy stomach turning over. I wished I hadn't dug out that diamond ring.

"Your hair is so fine," Palesa was saying, massaging my scalp as expertly as my old nurse Kaia had ever done. "This ivory color—is it natural?"

"Yes," I replied, somewhat surprised. "The black was a dye, to disguise my appearance."

"She means," Thanda put in, "we wondered if it came from being frightened. There's stories like that, of people going through terrible grief and coming out with their hair turned white as an old granny's."

"I am *not* old, thank you," Zalaika said with considerable tartness. The silver threads in her black hair added drama and sparkle to my mind.

"Nobody said you were, Mama," Thanda replied blandly. "So, if it's not that, Ivariel, do all of your people have hair your color?"

"I didn't invite Ivariel to soak with us so you could badger her with questions," Zalaika said.

"It's all right." I splashed my face with water to remove the stinging soap, and opened my eyes. This I didn't mind talking about. "Dasnarians are all fair-haired, it's true, but my hair color is unusual. Just like my mother's and she's famed for hers. My sisters have hair that's much more golden in color."

"Sisters," Palesa murmured. "You have sisters."

"Two, yes. Inga and Helva, younger than me."

"And how old are you?" Thanda pressed, ignoring her mother's cluck of disapproval.

"I'll be nineteen on my next birthday."

They were all quiet a moment. "You're practically a child still," Zalaika finally said.

I returned her sorrowful gaze evenly. "I haven't been a child for a long time."

She nodded slowly. "I can see that."

"Do you want me to cut the black off for you?" Palesa asked, breaking the uncomfortable silence, fluffing my hair as she poured water through it. "I assume you're growing it out now, since you haven't dyed it again."

Was I? "I don't know. Ochieng asked me the same thing."

They exchanged looks, rolling their eyes meaningfully. "Men always like long hair," Thanda declared with some aggravation.

"Dasnarian men do," I agreed.

"All men." Palesa sounded both mournful and amused.

"My hair used to be very long," I offered. "It nearly touched the floor when I stood." Encouraged by their murmurs of surprise, I continued. "I'd wear it in these very elaborate styles, lots of braids, with pearls."

"The pearls would be pretty," Palesa observed. "The same color as your skin and hair."

"Contrast is better," Thanda argued. "We should put pearls in our hair, and give Ivariel those polished onyx combs in trade."

"Silly, she doesn't have any pearls here."

"But I do," I said. I had all the pearls I'd pried from the gloves and my old wedding bracelet, the ones Kaja hadn't traded into coin for me. "I'm happy to share them."

Palesa and Thanda squealed, but Zalaika intervened with a firm. "We'll discuss that."

"I think I would like you to cut off the black," I told Palesa, "if it's not too much trouble."

She smiled in delight. "It will be fun. Soon we'll have the festival of *kuachamvua* and we'll find a way to fix the combs in your hair. Ochieng will be dazzled."

Thanda clapped her hands, singing a few notes of agreement.

Chagrined, I realized that—in my terrible self-absorption—that I hadn't told them the news. They'd likely not heard yet. "Ochieng said the festival of *kuachamvua* might have to be canceled this year. News came from downriver."

They indeed hadn't heard, having come straight to the hot pool on finishing their final chores for the day. If I'd expected them to show the same consternation the men had, they reassured me with their calm and careful questions. They asked me to repeat the encounter with the messenger, then relaxed back in the water.

"I apologize that I didn't tell you right away," I said.

Zalaika waved a hand, dripping with water droplets. "It's important news, but hardly that urgent. We are not canceling the festival of *kuachamvua*, I can tell you that."

"But Ochieng and Desta said—"

Zalaika raised her brows, silencing me. For all the ways, obvious and subtle, that she was unlike my mother, she shared the ability to assert herself with the smallest gesture. "Are my sons the head of the D'tiembo family? Are my daughters, for that matter?" She glared owlishly at her daughters, who had the temerity to giggle like girls. Another vast difference: I never, ever would have dared laugh at my mother. "No," Zalaika told them. "Not yet. And while I yet breathe, we live our lives to enjoy and celebrate what we have—not to fear what we might lose. That is the D'tiembo way."

~ 9 ~

We soaked a while longer, speaking little after that. I found myself relaxing, the hot water soothing away all the aches of my recovering body. I'd worked more in the past couple of days since the rains finally stopped than I had since... well, since Kaja trained me so relentlessly at the Temple of Danu.

We only got out when the men called from beyond the rockfall, wanting their turn. Zalaika sighed heavily and stood, water sheeting off her strong, dark-skinned body. She bore lighter stretch marks on her hips and belly—and grinned when she caught me looking. Splaying her hands over the spider-webbing of the marks she nodded at me. "We all bear scars of one sort or another. May the ones you gain from this point forward be as joyfully acquired as these."

Drying off and dressing quickly, we passed the men, lounging in various attitudes of impatient waiting. Ochieng looked surprised to see me with his mother and sisters, but didn't detain me or castigate me for not waiting for him. Instead he exchanged good natured taunts with his sisters and brothers, each claiming the others hogged the bath more.

It involved a great deal of hooting and name-calling—and would never happen in Dasnaria.

"Come on," Palesa took my hand and dragged me toward her family rooms when we reached the house. "We have a little time while they're occupied. I'll trim your hair and that Ochieng will be sorry he ever called you an ikkap."

"I didn't know what that word meant," I confessed, going along. Palesa and her husband and four children had a set of five interconnected rooms, one of them set aside as a family gathering area. It was unoccupied at the moment, with her husband down at the hot pool and the kids off with Thanda's oldest daughter, helping to prepare the evening meal.

"You speak our language so well I forget you don't know all the words." She laughed at herself, spreading a white cloth over the grass floor, and setting a stool there. "Sit, if you will. Do you trust me?"

With my hair, which I'd chopped off myself with a knife and zero remorse? Sure. "Go ahead."

Using a comb made of ivory—which she showed me, saying it exactly matched my hair—and very sharp small knife, she set to work trimming. The black ends floating around me like feathers, drifting to the white cloth.

"An ikkap is a very large fish that finds the shallow pools in the eddies of the river," she explained. "They're fat and lazy, sometimes not stirring from that spot for days. When he was a boy, Ochieng decided Thanda and I were like the ikkap for soaking in the hot pool so long. He was a *very* bad little brother." But she laughed as she said it, so I didn't tell her what a truly bad brother did to his sister.

Instead I asked, "What was Ochieng like as a boy?" surprising myself with my sudden curiosity.

"Bad!" She shook her head as she laughed. "Not really. But mischievous. Always getting into my and Thanda's things and giving them to the elephants. He said they looked prettier wearing our scarves and sparklies than we did. And his stories! Oh, that boy could make up stories from the moment he learned to talk. Before he learned better, he lied dreadfully."

I caught my breath a little. "He was dishonest?"

Palesa had moved in front of me, trimming the hair around my face, and paused, frowning. "Not like you mean. I think it was more that he imagined everything so vividly that his stories became as real to him as the truth."

"Oh." It still didn't sound good.

"He grew out of it, Ivariel," she said, lowering her comb and knife, holding my gaze. "Never worry about that. You won't find a man with more integrity and honesty in all of Chiyajua, maybe in the whole world."

I nodded at her, uncertain why that made my throat knot up as if I might cry. If she noticed, she pretended not to, studying my face and carefully shaping the fringes around it. Only bits of white fell now, like the snowflakes of my wedding journey sifting to cover the black.

What would this third face I wore be like?

* * * *

Palesa loaned me one of her shifts—if you can call insisting I put it on as "loaning"—one in a blue she said matched my eyes. When I protested that she'd already given me clean clothes, she rolled her eyes at me. "Pretty new hair deserves a pretty new dress. Oh! And a little bit of cosmetics, too. You'll be so beautiful my brother won't know what to do with himself."

Matchmaking, I realized. They all were, not-so-subtly, pushing Ochieng and me together. That could be part of his reason to want to marry me. Here all of his siblings had been married for some time, with children— and even grandchildren in Palesa's case—and he'd remained a bachelor. It would've been unthinkable in my family, so I could imagine that they'd told him the time had long since passed for him to take a bride. Zalaika had said something along those lines.

That would mean I'd been convenient. It could be that Ochieng had exhausted the possibilities in Nyambura and the surrounding communities, not finding a woman to his taste. He'd met me on a sailing ship and invited me to visit his home. He might've had this plan all along. From the moment he saw me, he'd said.

Of course, at that point, he hadn't realized what damage lay beneath the attractive surface.

So, I nearly balked, feeling like I shouldn't encourage his attentions—and his family's persuasions—by prettying up for him. But Palesa had been so kind that I couldn't find it in me to refuse further. I came very close to asking her why she thought Ochieng wanted to marry me. But, though the questions tumbled against my lips, I stilled them with silence. I maybe didn't want her to confirm my theories. Being honest with myself turned out to be quite an effort.

Palesa shooed me along, saying she would check on the children. When I emerged, Ochieng looked up from the *biah* he sipped with Desta and a few of the other men. His face went still. Setting the *biah* down, he walked away from Desta while his brother was still talking, not seeming to hear him call after him. Ochieng came straight to me, taking my hands gently, an arrested expression on his face. The men laughed at some remark of Desta's and I blushed.

Ochieng didn't give them a moment's attention—it was all on me. "I feel like I'm seeing the real you," he breathed in wonder, eyes wandering over my face. Then he winced. "That probably sounded all wrong. I meant that…" He didn't finish, searching for an explanation. My Ochieng, at a loss for words? Perhaps Palesa had predicted correctly.

"I know what you meant," I said, because I did. One by one, my disguises and layers of protection were falling away. All I'd need to look like the person I'd been all my life was to grow my hair long, wear a few more jewels, and lose quite a few scars. But that was surface, and who I'd become inside—this third self—couldn't ever be restored, certainly not as easily as trimming my hair and painting my lips.

Ochieng squeezed my hands lightly, sobering, his touch careful, as if he read my thoughts. "Come and have some *biah*? I understand the meal will be ready soon, such as it is."

With that cryptic remark, he tugged me to join them, pouring me a cup of the cold and sparkling brew also. The other guys nodded at me, then returned to their conversation. Ochieng led me down the terrace a short distance, then held up his mug in a private toast between the two of us. "To finding our real selves."

I clinked my mug against his, automatically replying in Dasnarian. "What does that mean?"

"It translates as 'true are your words.' A traditional Dasnarian reply to any toast that isn't an insult." I smiled at him and he returned it. Companionably we drank our *biah* in the last of the sunlight, slanting from the sun setting behind the butte.

* * * *

We ate out on the terrace that evening, the first time since the rains ended. As a family, that was, as we'd all been grabbing food between tasks and sitting out in the sun as much as possible. Then it took me aback, that I'd thought of us as a family—and me a part of it.

I sat cross-legged on the still warm stones, Ochieng on one side and Ayela on the other. She and the other kids had done a fantastic job making something of a feast for us. It was nothing on the scale of the welcome feast they'd all made when I first arrived—a welcome for Ochieng, not me—but they'd taken advantage of foods that had been hoarded in case the rains lasted even longer, and could now be replenished. The dishes also seemed more fun somehow. Lots of sweets and fancy breads, and bite-sized savories.

"We call this the 'children's feast,'" Ochieng said, reaching across me to tap Ayela on the nose. She blinked sleepily at him, smiled, then yawned in a jaw-cracking O. "Because all the adults are so busy, the kids do the cooking, and they get to make whatever they want. Which tend to be their favorite foods. We'll get back to having better meals soon."

"I like it." Bemused, I surveyed the array of foods on my plate. In the seraglio, we'd had no distinction between food for children and food for women. But then, we also hadn't had many formal meals, as such. My sisters and I had met for breakfast most mornings, from the time we became young women with earnest intimacies to share. Occasionally we'd had guests, or special celebrations. For the most part, however, we'd simply snacked on tidbits the serving girls brought us. Enticing treats like these.

They'd fed us like children.

The realization rolled through me without much bitterness, however. Perhaps I'd used up most of my emotional angst for the day. Ayela leaned heavily against my arm, too tired to sit upright, so I shifted to let her lay her head in my lap. She smiled in her sleep.

"She's worn out," I said to Ochieng.

He tipped his head in acknowledgment. "Everybody is. These first days after the rains end—there's so much to do and everyone bursting with restless energy to do it. How was your bath?"

"Wonderful!" He laughed at my enthusiasm, and I wrinkled my nose at him. "It felt so good to get completely clean, all over, all at once—and then dry off!"

"So true. And you soaked with my mother and sisters, eh?"

I slid him a glance. Ochieng often made easy conversation, but he rarely asked pointless questions. "Yes," I replied blandly. Then waited.

He chewed his food, pretending to listen to some story Thanda's husband was telling, but I could tell he itched to ask me more. Probably he hoped I'd offer more, but I'd learned the business of extracting and keeping secrets from a master. Whatever he asked me next would give me clues to what he really wanted to know. I surprised myself by enjoying the game.

Whatever it was, he never got to it, however, because an argument broke out over the festival of *kuachamvua*. Zalaika raised her voice and put down her foot.

"We are having the festival of *kuachamvua*. One week after the rains stop, we *always* have this celebration and this year is no different."

"This year *is* different, Mama!" Desta's face had set into hard ridges. He gestured to Ochieng. "We've all heard the news from downriver and we know our family-that-was. History repeats itself. They will be coming to us to fill their storehouses."

"Perhaps we should," Thanda put in, silencing everyone with what was apparently an extraordinary suggestion. "Perhaps we should send them food and other supplies. We have plenty and it would be the kind thing to do."

Desta looked at her with disgust. "The *kind* thing? These are not kind people."

"No?" She sprang to her feet and stood nose-to-nose with him. "The little girls like Ayela—they are not kind? Or the babies in their cradles? What about the eldsters with no fire to sit by to ease their aching bones—are they unkind?"

Desta set his jaw, a gesture that reminded me of Ochieng, though he would never get so angry. Ochieng always smiled, always yielded the argument cheerfully. Something, I realized, I greatly valued about him. Feeling a burst of affection, I slipped my hand into his. He glanced at our hands, then my face, in surprise—then squeezed gently.

"If we send them supplies," Desta was saying with exaggerated patience, demonstrating how very little patience he felt, "then they will know we have plenty and they will come for it."

Thanda threw up her hands. "Because they don't know it now? Why are we worried about them raiding upriver then, if you're so sure they've forgotten us?"

"We have to be smart, not weak with sympathy," he shot back.

"No, we have to be the best of who *we* are, follow what *we* believe in, not become a reflection of them. What's important is what our intention is, regardless of the outcome."

"That is ridiculous, *meurra*," he shouted.

Beside me, Ochieng chuckled, surprising me. He leaned his head toward me. "It's always a bad sign when they trot out the childhood insults."

"What does '*meurra*' mean?" I murmured back just as quietly.

"A donkey," he told me in Common Tongue. "You know this animal? Very stubborn, thick skulled."

I suppressed a smile, though I could see it as an apt description of the strong-willed Thanda.

"Ivariel, what do you think?" Thanda rounded on me, making me very happy she hadn't caught me laughing at her. Everyone looked at me, and I had no idea what to say.

"What do I think about what?" I asked carefully.

"What would your people do in this situation?" Desta asked. I found it most interesting that he supported his sister in asking me, when he'd been railing at her a moment ago.

"I am only a woman," I explained. Which, it turned out, explained nothing at all to them. "Women are not involved in discussions of politics or war in Dasnaria," I clarified.

Thanda frowned at me, perhaps not believing me.

"But you know your people," Ochieng inserted, caressing the back of my hand with his thumb. "What do you think the men like your brother Kral would say?"

That was easy. "Attack," I said simply. They all gaped at me with various expressions of shock and horror. I wanted to laugh so I did. "In Dasnaria it doesn't matter if the children, the babes, women, and elders are kind. The warriors run the empire and they have no compassion, no mercy. Those are regarded as weaknesses to be eradicated. They would prepare for war—and likely attack first."

Thanda had finally closed her mouth, giving me a long and canny look. "So, you agree with Desta—we should not send help."

I looked back at her. Odd how some small moments bring clarity. A turn happened inside me, like changing the color of my heart. "I agree with you, Thanda," I said, "for I am no longer in Dasnaria. This is Nyambura."

~ 10 ~

It felt good to declare it. Even better, they all smiled at me in approval. Feeling like I belonged to a family again, that I'd earned their approval, fed something deeply hungry in me. And encouraged me to crave more.

"It is settled then," Zalaika announced. "Thanda will coordinate sending what we can spare downriver. Desta, you work on fortifications and a defense plan for the town. Perhaps working with other villages nearby?"

"Happily, Mama." Desta threw a triumphant glare at Thanda, who serenely ignored him.

Zalaika smiled. "Palesa will—"

"I will assist Desta in preparing a defense," Palesa interrupted. "We need to get the elephants back into training anyway, we should work to sharpen their skills. I noted a number of us were quite rusty when we rescued Ivariel."

"As you will then, Daughter mine." Zalaika inclined her head. "I noted myself in that battle that I am not the young woman I once was. I shall hand Violet over to you, to lead the herd."

"A moment," Ochieng said quietly. "Ivariel has been working with Violet."

"Ivariel can work with Efe. She's best with her anyway." Zalaika bestowed a fond smile on me and I nearly preened with pleasure.

"Yes," Ochieng persisted. "But Efe will not be ready for battle any time soon."

"I don't wish to fight anyway," I told him, pointedly, because he knew that. The look he returned clearly said he intended to push me on that.

Zalaika beamed at me. "I agree with your decision, Ivariel, and your priorities." Raising her brows in subtle reprimand at Ochieng, she breezed on. "I will plan the festival of *kuachamvua*. We are having it," she raised her voice. "People will be coming from all around to sing and trade. We have young people who've been waiting nearly a year to marry, and we will not put them off."

Something about that bothered me, but I couldn't put my finger on what. Ochieng, too, because he cast me an assessing glance, a faint line between his brows. "Then Ivariel and I shall work with the elephants also?"

"Don't be silly," Zalaika waved a hand at us. "You'll be busy harvesting and carving the poles for your addition to the house. There's a great deal to do to prepare for your wedding, and not much time to do it in."

Though the word was, of course, different than in Dasnarian, it still froze me as if a blade had sliced me from behind, a silent, silvery, and agonizing shock. Wedding. Another one being planned for me, and I'd been running headlong for it, so desperate for approval. Had I learned *nothing*? Idiot. I'd have no choice, no escape. My chest went tight, my vision darkening.

"Breathe." Ochieng squeezed my hand, rather hard, and I started, coming back to the here and now. He stared at me a moment longer, as if making sure of me, then pulled his gaze from mine. "Nothing has been decided, Mama. Ivariel and I will not be getting married yet."

"Don't be ridiculous. If you don't marry this *kuachamvua*, you will have to wait an entire year."

"Then I will wait," he replied evenly.

"And if there is war?" She pinned us both with a steely glare.

"Then we deal with it, if and when it comes," he said.

"You could learn from your betrothed. Already she plans not to fight, to protect the babies she'll carry."

Babies? Wait, no, I wasn't...

"Mother." Ochieng's voice held a warning, even as he stroked my hand. "There is time for that. Don't—"

"It is easy to squander time when it seems to lie all in the future. Soon enough you will find that most of your allotted time lies in the past and the future holds not so much."

"Are you talking about me or yourself?" Ochieng shot back, and she flinched, as if he'd flung a rock at her.

"Oh, Brother," Palesa murmured.

Zalaika drew herself up. "All right then. I'll speak of me. I am no longer young. I no longer have a husband to hold me at night. *This* is what I have." She spread her hands at the gathering, her eyes welling with tears and her voice wobbling. My mother would sooner have died than expose her emotions in such a way. If she'd even had emotions. "My own future

WARRIOR OF THE WORLD

dwindles with each passing year, but *you*—you are my future. I have been patient with you, Ochieng. All these years I've waited for you to find a wife to suit you. Now you've brought Ivariel here and you asked us to accept her into the family, which we did. Gladly!" She paused to smile at me through her tears. "When Ochieng presented you to us for approval that first night, I didn't hesitate. Why do you hesitate now?"

I looked from her to Ochieng. "That ceremony the first night?" I asked him in Common Tongue, so they wouldn't understand.

He rubbed his forehead, looking pained. "It's not like she's making it sound, but I did ask them to potentially accept you as a member of the family so you could stay here." He squeezed my hand, then seemed to realize he'd already been holding it tightly, backing off his grip, but staring at me fiercely. "I wanted you to stay here. And it would give us time. I only wanted time to..." He trailed off at whatever he saw in my face.

I was shaking my head, I realized. "It's too much," I whispered. In Dasnarian, but he no doubt understood. Sliding my hand from his grasp, I wiggled out from under Ayela, who never stirred, boneless in sleep. I managed to stand. Everyone stared at me, but I couldn't read their faces. Panic fluttered in my breast, cramping my heart. Drawing on manners hammered into me, I drew myself straight. "Please excuse me," I said to them all. They stared at me, uncomprehending. "I must withdraw."

Too princess. I didn't care. I began walking out of the circle of light. "Ivariel," Ochieng called. "Wait."

"No," I said, still in Dasnarian. My brain had forgotten it knew any other languages. Dark night had fallen and I could barely see—but there was the gate to the steps. I opened it and plunged through.

"Ivariel—not that way!" Ochieng was running after me, so I descended faster, finding the handrails, my feet knowing the way.

He yelled my name and other words, falling on me like a blizzard I hunched against, that drove me down and down, fast as I could go. Escape. I had to escape or they'd take me back. They'd force the bracelets on me, lock me up and then—No. No. *No.*

I ran. So many times I'd gone up and down these stairs on the way to the river, to the little beach. My refuge. My escape. I'd gone many times a day before the rains. The wood crackled under my feet, the whole structure shaking, the world coming apart around me.

My feet found their way, my dancer's balance warning me of something I couldn't quite grasp, the steps feeling as if they fell away.

And then weren't there.

I plunged down, a shriek ripping out of me. The steps, washed away by the rains, I recalled. Too late. Much too late.

Flailing I reached, grabbing something. Wood splinters and rock. My feet dangling in darkness. Stupid. So stupid in my panic. I was Efe, drowning in floodwaters because I hadn't been smart.

And then Ochieng's hands were around my wrists. Calling my name, breaking through the hysteria, he pulled and I climbed. Kicking against the rock wall beside me, I pushed up. He caught me in his arms, back onto the wooden steps higher up, pulling us back against the rock face, as if that would make us safer. He held me far too tight, his ragged breathing pummeling us both.

"I'm so sorry," I said. "I forgot. I forgot about the missing stairs."

"I don't understand," he panted.

I knew he didn't. How could it be that just the word "wedding" sent me into such an icy panic that I couldn't even breathe? I didn't understand myself.

"Can you say it in Common Tongue?" he asked, mastering himself enough to let me go a little.

I laughed. Oh. He didn't understand because I'd said it in Dasnarian. I tried to think of other words, and couldn't find them. I'd become silent again. And had started weeping.

"No, no, lovely Ivariel," he murmured, stroking my face, wiping the tears away. "Don't weep. My mother doesn't understand. I'll speak to her. A year is nothing. Two years. Five. Ten. A hundred. I'll wait for you."

I concentrated past the wall of emotion, groping for words. Kaja teaching me Common Tongue. Baby steps. "Why me?" I asked him.

He paused. I wondered if I still hadn't used the right language. "Why you what?" he asked.

"Why do you want *me*?" I asked.

"I told you already," he replied, sounding confused. "I love you. I have since those first days on the *Robin*."

"I don't believe you," I said. If I'd had better command of myself, of my tongues, I might have said that more politely. As it was it came out blunt, even scolding. My mother's sneer. Hulda at her cruelest.

With his lean, hard body all along mine, Ochieng's flinch rippled through me. He and his whole family, so physically expressive of every little thing they felt.

"Could we maybe not have this conversation on a staircase battered by storms that could drop us both to our deaths at any moment?" he asked.

I thought that over, as if it were a problem with real alternatives, options for me to weigh. Something in my head simply had stopped working correctly, and I was unable to make even that simple, obvious decision.

"Come back up, love," he coaxed. "I promise no one will ever make you do anything you don't want to."

I looked up at him, though I could barely see any of his face in the muffling night. Where was the moon? "You can't make that promise," I informed him.

"I can and do. Now come on." He tugged at me, easing me back up the steps, like he might direct Violet. I became aware that the structure shuddered under our footsteps, rocking and clacking against the rock face.

"What is holding up the stairs?" I asked.

"Not a whole lot," he replied, in a wry tone. "Which is why we're getting off them."

"I miss the beach," I told him, then felt foolish. I sounded like a child. Or a crazy person. The latter was probably accurate. And here I'd told Zalaika I hadn't been a child for a long time. Maybe I'd never *stopped* being one.

"The beach is still there," he answered me, as if it had been a reasonable thing to say. "We'll go there now, if you like, the long way around."

I shook my head and the stairs creaked. Something broke off and fell. "It will be dark."

"True." He sounded calm, but he picked up the pace. "In the morning then. We can start stacking all the wood that's fallen," he added under his breath.

And then we were at the top, Ochieng opening the gate and drawing me inside. He bent over, leaning hands on knees, breathing in and out, long and slow. The terrace was quiet and deserted, though lights shone inside through the gauzy curtains, blowing in the light breeze, and a few torches remained lit along the wall. Zalaika detached herself from the shadows and put a hand on her son's shoulder, gazing at me.

She gave me a little smile, patted Ochieng's shoulder, and went inside without a word.

I'd frightened him, frightened all of them. I might've killed not only myself, but Ochieng. My legs abruptly weak, I sat on the broad, low wall that encircled the terrace. Some stars pinpricked the sky, but they seemed dim and far away—nothing like how close and brilliant they'd been aboard the *Robin*, when Ochieng had told us all the stories embedded in the patterns. He sat beside me, not touching me.

"There is water in the air still," he said, fluttering his fingers to show something rising from the ground to the sky. "The sun pulls all the water from the ground, making the air full and dense. Once it dries, the stars will shine bright again."

That made a kind of sense. Funny how he always seemed to know my questions before I did. He was a good man. Palesa had been right about that. I'd likely never find a better one.

But I didn't deserve a man that good. And he didn't deserve a wife as unstable as those wooden stairs.

"I think I should leave," I said.

~ 11 ~

"Why is that?" he asked, seeming unsurprised by the change of subject, or my harsh declaration.

"I was always going to leave," I pointed out, the words coming back to me. "When you invited me here, you seemed to understand I couldn't stay. You never said you intended to trick me into staying forever, to wear me down into agreeing to be your wife."

He rubbed his hands over his face, then leaned his elbows on his knees, staying there. "It sounds so bad when you phrase it that way," he said through his fingers. "I swear upon your goddess that wasn't my intention. I hoped for that, yes, but I thought time would work its magic. That we had a connection, that we'd already become friends and we simply needed the opportunity to come to know each other better."

"Yet you introduced me as your wife, to your family."

"What?" He sat up straight and looked at me. "No. Not at all. As my betrothed, yes. That's all."

"It's the same thing." I cut a hand through the air to dismiss that silly argument, a gesture I recognized as my mother's. Unpleasantly so. Ah, Hulda, how she haunted me still. She would have plenty to say about—and punish me for—my getting myself betrothed without her knowledge or permission.

"Wait," Ochieng said, taking my hands. I tugged at them, but he held on, doggedly. "Let's clear up at least this bit right now. Why do you say it's the same thing?"

"Because it is. That is the way of things." My jaw ached a little from clenching it.

"Not in Chiyajua. Here a betrothal is simply a public declaration of interest. Of potential. A betrothed couple might marry, they might not. It's a way of saying to our friends and family 'this person is precious to me; please treat them as precious to you, also.' That is why I introduced you to my family that way."

The phrasing, the earnestness of what he said, choked me up a little, the ever present tears welling up. *Precious to me.*

He leaned his forehead to mine, and I realized I'd echoed the phrase aloud. "Yes," he said very quietly, with great warmth. "Precious to me."

Oh. Maybe that hungry part of me wanted this, too.

"Now is when you explain to me what betrothal means to you."

"In Dasnaria, the betrothal is a legal contract, the first of several to bind a wife to a man. When a girl's father and brothers agree to the betrothal, there is no going back."

"What if the girl doesn't agree?"

I laughed, watery with it. "There's not even a way to say that. In Dasnarian, the word for betrothal means a contract between men to decide the fate of a potential bride."

He stayed quiet a moment, then finally spoke. "I think your Dasnaria must be an admirable place in some ways, because she gave birth to you, the most amazing woman I've ever met, but I find I cannot like a land that has such vile customs."

Some proud part of me wanted to protest, to point out all that the Dasnarian Empire had that simple Chiyajua did not, but I couldn't. I simply sighed for the truth of his words.

"To make it perfectly clear," he said, when I stayed silent, "you are bound by no contract. You are free of all obligations."

"Then I can leave."

He hesitated, then sighed, an echo of mine. "Of course. You left before, didn't you?"

"You brought me back," I felt compelled to point out.

"True. But only to heal, I promise."

"I know." And I did know. "I think that, since I can't…marry you—" Danu, I had a hard time even saying the word. "Since I can't do that, I need to break our betrothal."

"All right." He had his eyes closed, hands relaxed, voice even. I'd hurt him. He worked hard not to show it, but I could tell.

"And I should leave," I reiterated.

He opened his eyes and searched my face. "Don't leave. Please stay."

"I can't." I hung onto his hands, trying to make him understand. "They agreed to let me stay because of the betrothal, because I'd be family. If I am not family, I don't belong."

"That's not true," he protested, but his stubbornness spoke, not clear thinking.

"Your mother would say so."

"She is not the only one who decides."

"Ochieng..." I felt helpless to make him see. "She won't stop. If I'm here, she'll think I should be your wife. If I'm here and not your wife, you won't look for another."

"I don't want another. I've waited all my life for you."

I understood why Zalaika despaired of Ochieng sometimes, with his romantic ideas. "She won't see it that way. She'll see me either as an obstacle to you finding a wife, or she'll keep pushing me—and we've seen what happens. Ochieng, I am not sane." I used the phrase they used to describe Efe, how she wasn't quite rational.

He narrowed his gaze at me. "You are not insane."

"Ochieng. I freaked out just now, forgot what language I spoke, and ran down a staircase I knew was broken. I could've killed us both. Those are not the actions of a sane person."

He laughed. Actually threw back his head and laughed at me. "Ivariel." He said my name with the same patiently instructive tone I'd used on him. "You reacted like a wounded person. Of course you temporarily lost two of the languages you've only recently learned. Don't you realize how few people can even learn another language? You've learned huge amounts in only a few turns of the moon. You're incredible. You might be the smartest person I've ever met."

I rolled my eyes at him. "Now I know you flatter me. I am ignorant and stupid beyond belief."

He studied me. "Perhaps I haven't flattered you enough. I've clearly failed to tell you all the reasons why I love you that you can say you don't believe me."

"I don't think I believe in love at all," I clarified.

He tilted his head in question. "At all? Ever? What about a mother's love for her baby?

"Nature," I said. "So the mother isn't tempted to bang the child's head against the wall when it won't stop crying."

A laugh escaped him before he sobered, frowning. "You're serious."

"Yes."

"You think your mother didn't love you."

My turn to laugh. "If you met Empress Hulda, you would not question this. My mother valued me, to an extent, so long as I was useful and did exactly as she bade me."

"Your sisters. You must have loved them, and they you."

I turned over that idea. How Inga, Helva, and I had clung to each other, how they'd wept for me. How they'd promised to wait for my return and how, even in the midst of my pain, shock, and terror, I'd thought of them and negotiated for a modicum of freedom for them. "Maybe," I allowed, "if any of us had known how to love each other, we might have."

"Your brother, Harlan," Ochieng offered immediately. He'd been ready with that one—and he nodded at whatever he glimpsed in my eyes. "When you speak of him, your face changes, your voice softens, your whole body. You speak of him with love."

Did I? That feeling inside, like warm sunshine on my face, but radiating from within, swelled and burst. "Harlan saved my life," I said, and I could hear the change in my voice. "He helped me when no one else would. He sacrificed everything for me."

Ochieng was nodding still. "Of course you love him."

"I barely knew him. When he was a baby and then for only a few days when we met again."

"Love isn't bound by time."

"I don't even know what that means."

He stroked his thumbs over the backs of my hands. "I think you do. You just need to be safe and quiet for a while, to find yourself again. Tell me something—do you like me at all? Care for me, even a little bit?"

Of course I did. Ochieng had also saved me. Perhaps I was like a pet cat, hiding from those who kicked at me, snuggling up to those who fed and petted me. As simple as that. Ochieng had begun to frown at my silence.

I reached up and smoothed my fingers over his cheekbone, then over his brow, testing the texture of his skin and the bones beneath. He smiled a little. Curious, and also enjoying the touch.

"I like you, Ochieng," I said softly, and you would've thought I'd said he was the greatest man anywhere, the way his hesitant smile bloomed. "But because I like you, I think you deserve a better woman than me."

"How about you let me decide what I deserve?"

"What kind of friend would I be to you then? Ayela thinks she deserves all the sweets she can stuff in her mouth, but that's not good for her," I teased.

He didn't laugh at that. Quite the opposite, he went very stern. "Ayela is a child. I am not a child." Something in the gruff way he said that stirred me.

"No," I replied slowly. "You are a man." And had I really thought of him as a man? He was so different from Dasnarian men. That had made it easy for me to be his friend, because he didn't always come across to me like the men I'd known. With his laughing, smiling, relaxed ways, I found he didn't frighten me as just seeing the Dasnarian soldiers had, much less Rodolf himself.

Experimenting, I dropped my hand to his shoulder, tracing the muscled lines beneath his soft shirt. He held very still, letting me explore. I tried to imagine his strong body against mine, pressing inside me...and went cold. I dropped my hand, shaking my head to dispel the chill.

"I still don't know that I can ever be your wife in truth."

"Then be my wife in every other way."

I lifted my gaze to his, incredulous, but he looked utterly serious. He nodded at me. "I mean it. If you feel you can't stay unless you're my wife, then let's please the family and marry at the festival of *kuachamvua*. We can make our addition and share a room, but the rest can wait until you're ready."

"If I'm ever ready."

"If you're ever ready. We can live like brother and sister—but without the name-calling." He grinned at me and I smiled back, hesitant.

"Your mother will expect babies," I pointed out. "Living like brother and sister will not make babies."

"Even my mother acknowledges that there are powers of nature beyond her control. Not every couple makes children, and certainly not right away."

Children. The idea blazed through me. I might have a child, a mix of Ochieng and me. How might they look? I suddenly desperately wanted to know. "If I became your wife, you would have the right to my body, no matter what I wished," I said. That might be a solution, for him to simply plant his seed in me and ignore however I might scream or weep.

Ochieng took me by the shoulders, his grip fierce. "I want you to look at me and hear this, Ivariel." He waited for me to meet his gaze. "I will never touch you in that way unless you ask me to. I swear until the end of time."

I pressed my lips together, determined not to cry again. "I thought you said love isn't bound to time."

"Exactly." He smiled. Ochieng's "exactly," a kind of celebration of exactitude and serendipity combined.

"What's involved in this ceremony?" I needed to know if I could even make it through that.

"Very simple," he assured me. "In the family, building the room is the most important step. At the festival, we dress up. We promise to love and honor each other. Everybody sings." He laughed at my smile. "Of course. And then we dance. You'll like that part."

"No ring—no wedding bracelets?"

"No, my love." He caressed my cheek and I surprised myself by leaning into his palm. "We do not shackle each other. Only promises, nothing more."

Only promises. I could maybe do that.

"And, if you decide you don't like being married to me, you can always dissolve the marriage and leave."

That surprised me enough to have me lifting my head. "How's that?"

He shrugged a little. "Most married couples renew their vows to each other every morning—or every evening, depending on their personal custom. It's a way of committing to being there, in the marriage together. You can always decide not to renew."

"Or you. If you decide I'm entirely too crazy, you could decide not to recommit."

"True." He nodded gravely. "Though you should not hope too hard for that, as I'm highly unlikely to ever walk away from you."

Hope. A funny thing, that. I'd realized early on—back in those first dark days on the *Valeria*—that I didn't know how to hope for something for myself, that I'd have to practice, starting with small, simple hopes, and work my way up to wanting a direction for my life. Perhaps I could choose this. Try it on, like I'd tried to be a Warrior and Priestess of Danu.

"All right," I said. Then had to take a deep breath, my chest tight with both hope and dread, intertwined like a flowering vine creeping through a lattice of marble. "After all, I managed to be a pretend Priestess of Danu, why not be a fraud of a wife, too?"

He laughed, too pleased with me to be insulted. Or to heed that warning.

~ 12 ~

Ochieng worked some sort of magic whereby he informed his family that we would marry at the festival, but that I was shy on the topic and did not care to be congratulated—or even discuss it much. They mostly restrained themselves, giving me beaming and knowing smiles. Even the children refrained from saying anything, although they visibly shimmered with excitement and began calling me Mem Ivariel.

They did not, however, restrain their questions about learning the martial forms I'd begun to teach them before my injuries. With the cleanup work more or less under control—and everyone thinking about the possibility of attack—the parents asked me to resume lessons. The children met me on the terrace, my original five students, plus three more.

I tried to get away with simply teaching them the dance steps, to build strength and agility, to imprint the patterns of movement on their bodies, but they would have none of it.

"Why can't we work with the pretend weapons we earned?" Femi wanted to know. "Ayela did before."

True, and that had perhaps been a mistake on my part. The ducerse is a strenuous dance, which is why Kaja picked it as the primary one to adapt to my martial training, one that demands strength, balance, fluidity, and knowing where your hands are at all times. This is more difficult than it sounds. When I learned the ducerse, I practiced with round beads on my palms. With the fingers pulled back and the hand flat, only the dancer's balance and awareness keeps the beads from falling as she moves. Once I could do the entire dance at speed, my mother rewarded me with the two perfect pearls I danced with from then on.

Until I gave them to Rodolf as a wedding gift, but that didn't bear thinking about.

When Kaja adapted the dance, she'd said I could do it almost exactly the same as I'd always done, but with knives in my hands instead of balanced pearls. She'd argued that the dance was perfectly suited to attack and defense, and even theorized it had once served that purpose. I couldn't imagine a time or a world where women would have trained in the ducerse to fight rather than to refine their beauty in the seraglio, so I'd laughed at her.

Having seen much more of the world since, I began to wonder if she hadn't been correct.

Still, the most difficult part for me to learn had been to hold the blade in a closed hand, especially when it met resistance. I'd trained so diligently and for so long to keep my palms open and upraised, that my instincts had been to relax my hands.

So, when young Ayela, perhaps even better than I'd been at her age, especially considering she'd just learned the dance, had made it all the way through at speed without dropping a bead—the first of my students to do so—I'd presented her with a blunted metal dagger Ochieng had helped me craft from a kitchen knife.

The first thing my students did that morning when we resumed classes was demonstrate that all of them—even the three new ones—could do the ducerse without dropping a bead. They'd practiced all the rainy season, teaching each other. Yes, they needed some refinement, particularly leg work to deepen the knee bends, and to increase tempo. And I'd never tried to teach any of them the aspect of the dance where you wear bells and keep them utterly silent until you allow them to chime, building to a crescendo of sound. Still, they'd met the standard and deserved a reward.

Ayela even had her child's weapon thrust through a leather belt, one that looked very like my own sword belt, hidden away in my things. The D'tiembos must've retrieved that, too, because Rodolf had taken it from me, had taken all my weapons but one. Kaja's knife she'd had sent to me upon her death, asking me to plant it where it belonged. Had they left it in him? And how had they found my weapons among all those the Dasnarians had brought? I felt sure they had, because they'd been cleaned and laid out for me—before I hid them away.

"All right," I conceded. "I will see to getting you all *blunted* weapons."

"And real ones?" Ayela asked, a bloodthirsty glint in her lovely brown eyes.

"We will see," I replied. "First you all must build leg strength. No maybe bending knees. All of you practice together, going deep as you can. Like this." I showed them, beyond relieved that my old muscle habits responded, allowing me to skim through the deep, long lunges and rise again with grace. They needn't know how my knees and thighs screamed in protest. I had practice to do, too.

"May we sing?" One of the other girls asked. "Like we did when you danced during the rains?"

Why not? "Yes. But put most of your attention on strength, precision and speed, not on making pretty songs." I frowned sternly at them, much as Kaja had done to me. But they were not so easily intimidated as I had been, and sang out happy agreements.

As I hoped, Ochieng had not yet left the house, still scavenging for breakfast in the outdoor kitchen. I suspected he might not be an early riser, and it struck me that I'd discover this soon enough. Sharing a room. With a man. I couldn't even imagine.

Though I could recall how Princessa Adaladja had looked when she said she missed sleeping with "her Freddy." Perhaps it would be pleasurable. A happy thought.

"Good morning, lovely Ivariel." Ochieng picked up my hand, kissing the backs of my fingers with extravagant finesse, as some did in the Twelve Kingdoms—and making me laugh. "What is that smile for?"

"You and your silly games."

"Ah, but you were smiling when you walked up, thus inspiring my demonstration of affection. Laugh at me if you must." He put a hand over his heart dramatically. Palesa threw a fruit at him, but he caught it, grinning at her and biting into it with relish.

"I wondered if you could help me find and blunt more practice blades for my students," I said. "Like we did for Ayela." Months and forever ago. I remembered the elaborate pantomime I'd gone through, indicating what I wanted without speaking, Ochieng watching me with intense attention.

He remembered, too, because his smile took on a certain intimacy. "Of course. Come with me."

He led me to one of the store rooms bordering first room, finding a chest there. It was filled with daggers of varying sizes, all fine weapons to my inexperienced eye. "A shame to blunt these," he commented, "but you could select some now for when you move them into using edged weapons."

"I don't know that I will," I demurred.

He cast me an opaque glance over his shoulder. "Not to sound like Desta—and if you repeat me to him, I'll find a way to take revenge—but conflict is coming. If not this season, then next. These children you teach will need to wield edged weapons, if they are to protect what's precious to them, what's precious to us all. I think you understand this."

I did, but I didn't like it. With a sigh I began sorting through the contents, picking out daggers of varying lengths so the children could try them. I tried not to touch them, to let their hilts slide into my grip where they might feel entirely too familiar.

"Just keep the whole chest," Ochieng said. "Everyone else has their own weapons. Here, these might do for blunting. Some are beyond sharpening, so can be adapted readily." He slid them into a sack, then returned to looking for more.

"Ochieng?"

"Yes, my love?"

It warmed me that he'd taken to calling me that, as if he might make me believe it if he repeated it often enough. It might be working. "How did you find my weapons amid all the others, when you rescued me from the Dasnarians?"

"I didn't so much. Once I found where you'd dropped, I bandaged you to stop the major bleeding and took you to the healer. The others who stayed to make sure all of the intruders were dead went around and collected all of the armor and weapons, before they scattered the naked bodies for the scavengers. Here, that should be plenty."

I found it faintly horrifying to hear my easygoing Ochieng so matter-of-factly discussing feeding the bodies of my erstwhile countrymen to the wild animals. But then—he hadn't told me until I asked.

"Once you were sleeping and we'd all recovered," he continued, rising from his crouch, "I sorted through everything they'd brought back and found your personal weapons. They were easy to differentiate from the rest. I cleaned them up and set them aside for you. Why, are you missing something?"

Completely bemused, I couldn't decide what to ask first. "You brought back *all* the weapons and armor?"

"Excellent metal. We weren't going to leave it for the oasis ruffians to capitalize on."

"And then scattered the bodies."

"We wanted to be sure that if anyone did search for them, there wouldn't be much to find. And the animals need to eat, too." He flashed me a grin, an edge to it that reminded me of the bloodthirsty glint in Ayela's eyes. How had I missed this side of them before? He sobered, searching my face. "Isn't that what you wanted—to have them effectively disappear, victims of hubris and the rainy season?'"

"Yes," I replied, which I had, but the details somehow made it that much more brutal. I shouldn't feel sorry for them—many of those men killed by my own hand—but for a Dasnarian man to be fed to the wild animals, devoid of his armor and weapons... Unthinkable. "What of Kaja's blade? I don't recall seeing that."

"Ah." He looked thoughtful. "That—we left where you planted it, as your mentor wished. It seemed..." His dark gaze stayed steady on mine, careful of my reaction. "Sacred, in a way. Important to leave there. We buried him like that, so the blade would forever pin him to his unmarked grave. Then we salted the earth and had the elephants trample it flat, the dirt packed so tightly it would not erode in the rains."

The small hairs on my neck pricked. A lethal edge to this man I thought I'd known. "Do you believe the dead can rise from their graves?" I asked him.

Instead of laughing that off, he pursed his lips. "Whether I believe such a thing or not, I would take far greater steps to ensure that monster never again walks this earth."

He said it so evenly, so without inflection, that I knew great emotion lay beneath his words.

"Thank you," I whispered, wishing I could say more.

Relaxing slightly, he moved close to me, touching my cheek in a light caress. When I didn't jump away, when I leaned into him, he wrapped his arms around me in a gentle embrace. "I would've gladly killed him for you. I sometimes have dreams of doing so."

"I'm glad you didn't."

A dark laugh fluttered in his chest under my ear. "So you could have the satisfaction."

"No." No matter that I'd wanted Rodolf's death, I hadn't wanted to deal it. "So you can be free of this."

"I won't ever be. I don't want to be. It's part of who you are, thus also mine."

Leaning against him in the quiet shadows of the storeroom, his heart thudding under my ear, I smiled at the way his words sounded like a vow.

"Do you want the blade back?" he asked into my silence. "I can find the grave and the elephants will help me dig."

Gruesome to imagine. "No. I think you did right to leave it there. Kaja would've liked that."

He ran a hand over my hair, feathering his fingers through it. "Good."

"Besides, the elephants have better things to do than dig up what's best left buried."

Setting me away from him a little, he smiled at me, looking for my meaning. "Shall we begin carving our poles?"

"Yes. This afternoon?"

"Yes." He brushed a kiss on my forehead, and I closed my eyes to savor the sweetness of it. Rodolf lay moldering in an unmarked grave, Kaja's blade forever through his heart, and I lived. Better, I thrived, a strong and kind man's lips on my brow, his breath warm on my skin. I stayed still for it. Ever so gently, Ochieng placed kisses on my eyelids, making me breathe a sigh, then on either cheek. Wanting more, I tipped up my mouth, to receive his kiss there, too.

Sacred. And right.

~ 13 ~

After I dismissed the children, I went to work with Efe for a while. All of the younger elephants were skittish and recalcitrant, having been left to their own devices during the rains. Old veterans like Violet had stepped back into work with alert interest, as if they'd grown as bored as we had with little to do. The young, however, had to be gradually coaxed back into their training routines.

Efe, in particular, had reverted considerably. More than ever she reminded me of myself, retreating back into my silences and aloneness. Not even Ochieng had tried to ride her yet, saying she needed time to get used to being around people again. Mostly I was supposed to visit her—buried in mud to her eyeballs more often than not—and to give her treats, to remind her people could be good parts of life. I wouldn't tell Ochieng as much, but I found myself using the same techniques on her as he did on me: undemanding affection, quiet understanding, and plenty of sweet words.

There were good reasons Ochieng had managed to domesticate the wild thing I'd become as much as he had.

Ochieng had been conferring with Palesa, discussing the various elephants of the tribe and assigning them the best riders to work with. When he finished—and I gave up getting Efe to come out of the lagoon, though she did lever up enough to tuck the fruits I brought her into her mouth—he took my hand and led me to the storehouse.

As we arrived, the workers were just lowering a large tree trunk from the top level, using ropes and pulleys. Hart gave me a jaunty salute, and several of the workers made ribald comments, so I figured everyone knew what the trunk was for. I refused to be embarrassed. Or rather, to reveal how self-conscious I felt. It reminded me of some of the discussions around me during my wedding celebrations, when the men had spoken to each other about my deflowering. Despite the theoretical knowledge I'd had then, I understood much better now what they'd referred to. If I thought about it too hard, that dark anger stirred, that they'd laughed about it.

I hadn't been a person to them, and that wound remained unhealed. But this joking wasn't unkindly meant, so I resolved to look past it, and gave Ochieng a reassuring smile when he touched my hand in silent question.

I studied the trunk as they laid it on the ground and unhooked the ropes from it. It had been stripped of the major branches before we'd ever floated it downriver, mostly courtesy of Violet and Bimyr, who'd done the heavy work of uprooting the tree in the first place. That had been a good day, when Ochieng took me to the forest to see how the elephants worked together. Once they'd brought the tree down, the humans had sat for a picnic, while the elephants stripped the tree of all the delicious goodies. Then Ochieng had marked the tree with the D'tiembo symbol and the elephants had carried it in tandem to dump it in the river to later fetch up on the weir downstream.

I'd missed that part, when the D'tiembo workers had pulled the tree out and stored it, because that's when all the terrible news arrived.

Ochieng picked up my hand and kissed it. "That was a good day," he said, with a warm smile.

"And bad," I reminded him.

"More good though. Our first kiss. The first time you spoke to me. Our tree."

I had to laugh. "Perhaps more good than bad then."

"Let's move this to a place we can work on it." He glanced around and saw Capa, one of the younger elephants not currently training with Palesa, loitering around—and considering getting into trouble by trying to steal some fruit, by the gleam in her eye. Hearing Ochieng's signal, she ambled over, trunk skating over the ground in curiosity.

"Hup, hola, ho," Ochieng sang, some of the workers singing it back, weaving into the bright sunshine of the day, and my surprisingly happy mood. I'd successfully set aside the dark thoughts, so that had to be a good sign. Capa eyed the tree, dusting it with the tip of her trunk, then wrapping her trunk almost delicately around a smooth spot.

"Don't we need two elephants to carry it?" I asked.

"Naw—Capa can drag it the little ways we have to go. The path is all cleared off." Ochieng put a hand under the corner of her jaw and began walking. He guided her around the bluff—not the direction I expected— and to the little beach.

Of course he'd remembered I'd wanted to visit it. At the base of the bluff, the stretch of fine gravel formed a crescent along the side of the river, free of the tall grasses and shrubs that otherwise blurred the margin between water and land. The shape of the beach had changed since I saw it last, reworked by the floods, and littered with various bits of detritus. But the sun shone warm on the rocks and the peaceful feel of the place felt like a kind of coming home.

Which it could be. If—when—I married Ochieng, I would be part of this family and this place for the rest of my life.

As Ochieng guided Capa to a clear area, I looked around for evidence of the wood I'd heard falling—and spotted Ayela and Femi gathering the pieces and neatly stacking them against the cliff side. High above, the steps dangled, looking exceptionally precarious.

"I thought the kids could start salvaging the wood," Ochieng said, following the direction of my gaze. "I didn't want to donate more to the river than necessary."

"I'm sorry about that," I started to say, but he threw me an affectionate smile.

"Don't be. Sometimes the pus has to be squeezed out before the wound can heal." He directed Capa to drop her load in a smooth area well above the water. With a pat on her flank, he thanked her, and she happily waded into the river. "You should see if Efe wants to come watch."

"Now?"

"Sure. I need to smooth this trunk before we can start in earnest. See if an excursion to the river can coax her out of her mudhole." He pulled a hatchet from his belt and began chopping at the nubs of the broken-off branches.

"All right." I waved to Ayela and Femi, then went back down the path that wended its way along the river's edge before going back inland to skirt the elephants' lagoon. The mud there remained exceptionally sodden, squeezing between my toes, and the grasses had grown in leaps since before the rains. They waved above my head in places, bright green, and full of life.

The river flowed full and sluggish now, bloated with rain and satisfied with herself. Ripples glittered in the sunlight, with great flocks of waterfowl descending in waves to skim along the surface, then settle in to glide with the minimal current. Life returning to normal in the wake of the storms.

I caught a glimpse of something else, something bigger on the water, and shielded my eyes against the glare. A formation of long, narrow boats, rowing upstream against the current, remarkably fast for all that. People from town? I hadn't seen them use boats like this before, but—

Something whistled toward me, and I dodged. An arrow thudded into the ground a hands-breadth away. All my senses—the well-honed instincts of the victimized—screamed into high alert.

Capa in the river. The kids gathering wood. Ochieng. Ochieng. Ochieng.

I ran, fast as I could, ducking low though my white hair and colorful gown no doubt shone like a flag. A few more arrows flew around me, but I ignored them. I needed to get to Ochieng.

Two of the boats were outpacing me. I rounded the bend. Ochieng on the beach, back to the river as he straddled our wedding log, chopping at the nubs of branches. Capa in the river showering herself with water.

I shouted. No words, just a warning, a scream of despair. Ochieng looked up in surprise, the lines of his body going tense. At the same moment, Capa sent up a trumpet of pain as an arrow thudded into her flank.

Ayela screamed in fury, a tiny warrior running down the beach to the water, knife glinting in her hand, Femi right behind her.

"No!" I yelled, impotently, heart hammering so loud in my ears I couldn't hear myself.

Ochieng yelled something at the kids and splashed into the water, where Capa flailed, trumpeting her pain and rage. In the distance, other elephants answered. Ochieng climbed Capa's tall body like a tree, wheeling her around. She fought him. Another arrow hit her, perilously close to where Ochieng lay on her back, and she reared.

He got through to her somehow, and she wheeled, coming down on the boat nearing her. It cracked open, spilling men into the water. The other boat neared the shore and two men leapt out, dragging it onto the sand.

I stood, rooted, paralyzed, empty-handed. Unable to make myself do anything at all. Blood streaked down Capa's sides, swirling into the water. Ochieng urged her into interposing her bulk between the kids and the attacking men.

Kaja would have charged into the fight. Kaja would have been wearing her sword. She wouldn't have left it packed away, useless, in the house. Good Danu, the house. Smoke billowed up on the top of the bluff, an acrid stench in the balmy air. I should do *something*, but I had no idea what.

Ayela screamed. One of the attacking warriors had lifted her off her feet. She kicked his jaw, impressively knocking his head aside before he tossed her through the air. She landed in a crumple and he turned his attention to Capa's wildly swinging trunk.

And I was running again. Dimly I heard Ochieng's shouting. Elephants trumpeting. Blood in the water and fire in the sky. Ayela, having regained her feet ran toward me, tears pouring down her face. Femi lay on the sand unmoving. No, oh no.

Catching Ayela, I pulled the knife from her hand. Not the blunted practice blade, but one of the Dasnarian daggers I'd gotten from Ochieng only that morning. Plenty sharp. "Go!" I shouted at her. I pointed upriver. "Run and hide."

"Femi!" she sobbed.

"Run," I repeated. "Run fast!"

I turned to the battle. The noise and panic had receded from pounding around my temples. Cold, clear, and eerie silence wrapped around me. And inside, that serpent of hatred raised her head and flared her hood, waking from deep sleep.

~ 14 ~

"Ivariel."

I knew that voice. A good sound. I stood in a river of blood, eyes watering from choking smoke, screams in my ears. No. Oh no.

"Ivariel. Please, I need your help."

I blinked away the moisture, then went to wipe a hand over my face. A grip on my wrist and I spun, lashing out with the blade I hadn't known was in my hand. The man ducked, matched my spin, and came up behind me, arm wrapped around my waist, body cupping around mine—and my wrist in his fierce grip out to the side.

"Ivariel!" His voice came harsh and panting in my ear. "I need you. Come back to me."

My hand hurt from gripping the dagger so hard, my wrist straining as I fought to free myself.

"La, Ivariel, steady now," Ochieng crooned. Ochieng. My Ochieng.

I let go of the knife.

He let out a long breath, laying his cheek against mine. "Are you all right?"

I nodded.

"Words, please."

"I am here," I said.

"And in a language I know?"

I might have laughed at the absurdity, but blood swirled around me, a river of it. Concentrating, I reached for the words. "I'm fine, but what about Femi?"

With a gust of relief, Ochieng let me go, turning me to look into my eyes. Then nodded crisply at whatever he saw. "Stay with me, all right? Femi is lost to us. I need your help with Capa."

I looked around, able to see beyond the screaming images in my head, and took in the scene. Bodies of the foreign warriors floated in the water, or half-draped across the sand. Femi's little body lay where I'd last seen it, when I told Ayela to run. Capa… the big elephant lay on her side in the water, blood flowing out and mixing with the attackers' turning the river red where I stood in it calf-deep.

"What do you need me to do?"

"Here." He pulled me to her, and I only then noticed the barely concealed desperation in him, how carefully he'd cloaked his panic with calm in order to deal with me. "Press down to staunch the bleeding." He arranged my hands around an arrow in Capa's upper leg, where blood pulsed out. "This is the worst. Can you stay with her while I get help?"

I nodded, an automatic response, though I wondered at the way she lay, with her head partly in the water. "Won't she drown?"

"She's all right lying down, she can breathe."

I noticed she held the tip of her trunk above water, like Efe did in her mud baths. Efe—had the attackers gotten to her? "Ochieng, there were more boats. The house—"

"Shh. I know. It hasn't been that long. I'm going to see and for help." He set the dagger on Capa's flank, handy to me. "In case you need it," he said.

"You take it."

"I have this." He held up the hatchet he'd been using, the handle streaked with blood, and for the first time I noticed he also was spattered with gore. "I'll be right back."

"I should go with you," I started to let go, but Capa's blood pulsed out, hot and bright over my hands, so I pressed down again.

"You're better here." Ochieng said this very firmly, giving me a long look. And I understood what he was saying—that if I went into a frenzy again, I could hurt someone not the enemy. "Capa needs you."

"I'll stay here," I said. "Ochieng, I—"

"I know." He saluted me with the hatchet, then took off running.

* * * *

I'd been through strange waiting periods in my life, but that afternoon vigil of kneeling in the bloody water—Capa's breathing soughing heavily, her blood seeping between my fingers—as the light lengthened was one of the strangest. For a while I stared at the dagger Ochieng had left for me, reconstructing the memory of taking it from Ayela, knowing the little brat had taken it without permission, sending her to run and hide... And then not much of anything.

The dark serpent that dealt death stirred, rearranging her coils around my heart. Ready.

Was it the blade in my hand that set her off? I didn't think so. Something else then, as had happened the night before when I ran down the steps. The difference then was that I hadn't had a blade to rend and tear.

Waiting there, I had plenty of time to survey the bodies. Which showed signs of Ochieng's hatchet, which had been unmistakably crushed by Capa's fury—and the many who looked to be dead from the dagger I'd wielded.

I wasn't sorry to have killed them, not as I sat in the water staining still with Capa's blood, the gentle elephant wheezing, the arrows piercing her in several places wobbling with each labored breath. She kept her trunk draped over her shoulder, but I began to be sure that she'd die under my hands. So I sang to her. Not Nyamburan songs, as none came to me, but a Dasnarian lullaby I used to sing to my baby siblings. Harlan had loved it and I tried to summon his gentle nature to soothe Capa.

Sleep baby sparrow, safe in your nest.
Sleep cozy kitten, at your mam's breast.
The wind blows cold, the wind blows mean.
But it can't touch you, and it won't chill me.
You have your nest, and I have my song.
And the sun that has set will rise before long.

Funny how the words all came back to me, and I sang it over and over, until my throat grew too dry. The smoke from the house seemed to be thinning, though I didn't know what that meant. The house itself wasn't visible from the beach, so it could be that everything had burned, the fire down to bare stone. It could be that the attackers had killed everyone, which meant they'd eventually find me and Capa. I supposed if that happened, I'd release the wound, take up the dagger, and give myself over to the serpent of destruction. Maybe I could kill a few more of them. It would do no good to save Capa only to leave her to the people who killed her.

As Capa's breath grew more labored, and the blood seeped ever more slowly, with barely any of the thrust it once had; it seemed she would die, regardless. I considered taking up the dagger and going to join the fight. Though I might hurt someone of the family. Which would be worse—to kill someone by my own hand or through my inaction? *What's important is what our intention is.*

I mentally debated the philosophical question, which is how it seemed: remote and very far from my odd suspension in time.

A scream rent the air, bringing me to alert. I wrenched my head around to see Ayela's mother, Nafula, running headlong down the beach, strong brown legs flashing as she held her skirts high to run fastest. She reached Femi and fell to her knees, sobbing. Capa groaned at the disturbance, and I sang to her, so she wouldn't thrash. My only job.

Nafula's husband followed soon after, and Palesa, gathering in a small and broken huddle. Then Ochieng was beside me, a leather bag slung over his shoulder. He gave me a smile, though it was grim, and set to work with a huge needle and sinew. Capa flinched, an all over body shudder at the first piercing of the needle, so I began to sing to her again and she calmed.

Tersely Ochieng had told me to move the pressure of my hands from here to there, holding flaps of tissue closed while he stitched them together like fabric. I was glad to have this task, at least, so I could be excused from those who carried Femi's limp body away from the beach.

"The good side to Capa being so far gone," Ochieng said, "is that she isn't fighting this. Your song helped. You did well. It's fortunate you're not squeamish. Help me with the rest?"

He hefted himself carefully over Capa's flank. She twitched her ear, rolling her eye to look at him, which I took as a good sign that at least she cared. "Bring your dagger," he called.

Gingerly, I took up the thing, holding it all wrong, because I was afraid that if I seated it properly into my hand then that other face would rise up and take me on a killing spree. I partly wanted that to happen, to go kill all of those who'd hurt us. Which made me distrust it all the more.

I followed Ochieng up the rise of Capa's flank, her wrinkled skin soft and the occasional spiky hair pricking through my light gown, she groaned and I apologized to her. Ochieng held out his hand for the dagger and I gave it to him hilt-first, and with relief.

"Sing your song, would you?" he asked, and he sounded so tired and dispirited that I obliged. I sang and he murmured instructions to me, having me hold an embedded arrow steady while he cut around it. He threw it to the beach, the fury in the power of the throw the only other sign I'd seen of how he felt inside. Allowing the blood to flow—brighter here, which had to be good, right?—a few breaths, he then sewed up this puncture too.

We repeated the surgery three more times, and Capa lay obligingly. Or too weak to protest. When we finished, Ochieng jumped off of her, then held up his hands to help me down. Keeping his arm around me, we waded onto the beach. He leaned heavily on me.

"Are you hurt?" I asked, abashed that I hadn't asked before. Ochieng always seemed so bright and powerful to me that it didn't seem possible for him to be wounded.

"No. Not in body," he replied. Then he sat, almost a collapse, and I went with him. We leaned against each other. Capa in the water before us. Our wedding log just off to the side. The shadows slanting long as the sun set behind the bluff, smoke staining the light bloodred.

~ 15 ~

"I should get up," Ochieng eventually said. "Go help the others."

"All right, I'll go with you."

But neither of us moved.

"Should we make Capa stand?" I finally asked. I hated seeing her like that, lying in the water like the corpses of the men we'd killed.

Ochieng shook his head. "Elephants are not like horses. It won't do her harm to lie down and rest. She'll stand under her own power or not. We've done all we can for her."

Oh. I nearly pointed out that he'd done all the work in saving her, but it seemed wrong. My hands had wrinkled from being so long in the water and Capa's blood. Dark crescent moons of dried death lay under the nails and I wished I could clean them. Or rather, that I could wish them clean.

As if reading my mind, in that uncanny way he had, Ochieng folded my hands in his, cupping them together like something fragile. *Precious to me.* "I liked that song," he said. "Dasnarian?"

"Yes. Harlan's favorite. He always called it the baby sparrow song."

"Can you translate it for me?"

I did my best, though the rhyme and cadence didn't come through. When I finished, he made an approving sound, and then we sat in silence. I realized how surreal this was. How we talked of nothing that had happened. I wasn't even sure what question to ask first.

Finally I spoke. "What happened?"

A general question—and one I obviously knew part of the answer to, but he didn't point that out. Not generous, patient Ochieng. He let go of my hands and smeared his own over his face wearily, speaking into them. "They were Chimtoan. Five more boats, besides the two that landed here.

Three stopped at other houses downriver, so far as we can tell. The other two banked just down from here and the warriors went to the storehouse. They split into groups—one to steal elephants by riding them away, another to raid the storehouse."

I listened to the grim recitation of losses. The injured were being cared for. The dead taken to be prepared for burial, including young Femi. Two elephants lost—two of the younger ones who hadn't been training. Not Efe, Violet, or Bimyr, a relief I felt terribly guilty for feeling.

"Efe stayed buried in her mud the whole time," Ochieng said with a half-laugh. "So I suppose she won a point on all of us there. I can only imagine if they'd come a little later—or if I'd gotten you to dig her out of her nest sooner."

"They could never have ridden her," I said, feeling the absurd humor of it. "She would've gone crazy and killed them." Like I had. The unspoken words hung between us. He looked at me sideways, long legs drawn up at the knee, long-fingered hands dangling between them, his face somber.

"If you're regretting that you lost yourself to that inner demon—don't. You saved my life, Ayela's, and Capa's."

I didn't say I hadn't saved Capa's life, not yet. "Did Ayela come back?"

"Back?" He cocked his head. "She was way ahead of me, calling warning."

Of course she had. "I told her to run and hide."

He smiled, a brief quirk. "Stubborn, that one."

"I don't understand why they shot Capa if they wanted elephants."

Sighing, he shifted his gaze to the elephant. "It's a technique of theirs. Confuse the elephant with arrows—see how they weren't all that long? Just enough to prick and agitate—then they climb on and urge them into a panicked run. Capa took that bad wound in just the wrong place to bleed out, because I used her to attack. She took a spear." He looked at me again. "You slit the throat of the man who did it."

I didn't remember. None of it. And I couldn't decide if that was a curse or a blessing. Because he watched me steadily for a reaction, I shifted the inquiry away from my crazed psyche. "Is the house gone?"

"Part of it. Thanda and some of the kids got it put out before it got too far. Wood and fabric. We live in a pile of kindling."

"Built on stone," I said, then felt silly because the stone hardly mattered.

But he took my hand again, smiling, a shadow of his usual sunniness in it. "Very true. All in all, we did not lose as much as we could have. Thanks in great part to you and your warning."

WARRIOR OF THE WORLD

"At least it's over with," I said, but he was shaking his head before I finished.

"No. If only. They didn't get away with much, and we know their ways from the past. This was a test. A strike force to assess our defenses and scope our stores. They took samples, to report back with."

Samples. They killed our people, kidnapped two of our tribe, and Ochieng called them samples. He squeezed the hand he held, then stood, drawing me with him. "It's good to be angry. We will need our anger for the days ahead. Help me push our wedding log into the river."

Stricken, I looked from him to it. He cupped my cheek, eyes full of grief now. "We will cut another, when this is done. This one has blood on it. Blood drawn in violence. I won't build our marriage on that."

So I helped him roll it into the river, downstream of Capa, and just far enough for the sluggish current to catch it and carry it away. We dragged the bodies of the enemy out there too, to wash downstream as a warning, though Ochieng doubted they'd heed it. More of them had gotten away than had died.

I agreed, because I knew very well what desperation could drive people to do.

Then we washed off the blood as best we could, though we'd only get soiled again. We had a long night's work ahead, to recover from the attack and brace for another. Everyone labored, even the kids, exhausted and covered in grime. No one spoke of the festival. Not even Zalaika, who bathed the body of her dead great-grandson, singing a mourning song that made my hair stand on end.

It occurred to me that it didn't matter what Ochieng and I carved our wedding poles from. Our marriage—if it occurred—would always be built on blood drawn in violence, desperation, and grief, because that was my fate and my destiny. It seemed I'd never escape what I'd been born to be. And whoever made contact with me would share in my curse.

* * * *

Just before dawn, I took Violet to visit Capa. Ochieng's suggestion, of course. We'd all been checking on Capa periodically—or sending one of the kids to do it—and she still lived, but hadn't yet gotten up. While it wouldn't hurt her to rest lying down, we all understood that whether she ever got up again would be a threshold moment.

Ochieng thought having the tribe matriarch with her might rally Capa's spirits. Efe had buried herself so utterly that only the bare tip of her trunk stuck out. Only by tickling her snout and feeling for her slow inhalations and exhalations could I verify she lived. If she hadn't come out later in the day, Ochieng had said, we'd have to dig her out and try to get her to eat and drink. And he'd fully intended to take Violet to Capa, too.

That was before he fell into exhausted sleep, in midargument with Desta. He'd sat down, tipped his head back, and went straight out. Thanda and I told Desta to do likewise—both men had gone gray from fatigue—and I eased Ochieng to lie down on the bench right there. It didn't wake him in the slightest to be thus rearranged, which said something.

I knelt beside the bench after Thanda left, looking down on Ochieng's sleeping face, something I'd never done before, watching a man asleep and vulnerable like this. With Harlan on our mad escape, though I'd known he slept, I'd been so weary from my injuries inside and out that I'd been absorbed with myself and never paid attention to his sleep. Even on the journey to Nyambura, when I'd stood watch, I'd had my focus outward, alert for danger, rather than looking at the sleeping men.

His face softened in his sleep, making him look younger, and I caught a vision of how our son might look as I soothed him into sleep. It burned like touching snow with bare feet, the longing for that to be possible. And in the same way, numbness soon followed, knowing that it simply couldn't be. Smoothing back the hair that had come loose from his queue, I brushed a kiss over his mouth, soft in sleep, making me feel all that much more tender.

Then I took Violet to Capa, which had been the last thing Ochieng had asked me to do. I rode Violet, as I hadn't since the night we rescued Efe, as I still found it easiest to direct her that way. When we came in sight of Capa, Violet picked up her pace, trotting to her fallen sister and nuzzling her, dusting her wounds with her trunk and making a groaning noise. Capa lifted her head a little, answering with a creaky moan, then lay back down again.

Violet stood over her, staring off into the pre-dawn gloaming, as if keeping watch for attackers. There could be predators, I supposed. The lions I'd seen, or the great toothy crocodiles Ochieng had told stories about. Perhaps that had been his intention in asking me to take Violet to Capa, which made me wish I'd complied sooner. Only there'd been so much work to do, so many wounded to tend. And Ochieng had seemed so uncharacteristically dispirited that I hadn't wanted to stray far from him.

Which made no sense, because what could I do? But still, I'd felt better when he finally slept.

Perhaps because I'd slept so much while I was healing, or because I'd spent the bulk of the time they were all fighting holding my vigil by the river with Capa, but I felt burningly awake. I couldn't imagine lying down and trying to sleep. Wading into the river, I dunked myself in the cool water, scrubbing at the grime as best I could. At least in the gray light I couldn't see if blood still washed away from me.

I didn't want to go back to the house, have to see its gaping wounds, smell the char, bear witness yet again to Femi's small, bloodless body and hear the weeping of his family. Cowardly of me, no doubt, but I felt emptied out and unable to face any more.

The shadows stirred, the mist of morning moving and reshaping. The large, shadowy forms began to join us. The other elephants, moving in a silence that rivaled my own—and that never ceased to astonish me—coming down to the river, touching Capa with their trunks, then wading in deeper. I'd seen them do this before the rains, standing in the river at dawn, raising their trunks to the rising light and trumpeting.

And it occurred to me to sing the prayers to Glorianna, as I hadn't done since that first day that the sun came out.

I didn't feel moved to celebrate as I had that day. Something else gripped me. A need to feel something other than despair. I waded to shore, against the tide of elephants, slipping between them and touching their questing trunks with my hands as we passed each other, exchanging our own greetings.

The light grew pink, the sky brightening, and more elephants arrived. More than our tribe, ones from the other Nyamburan families—and wild ones, including the great bull elephant I'd glimpsed only a few times, with his enormous tusks and grizzled hide. All up and down the river they appeared, making me glad so many still survived, and gripping me with terror that another dawn would change that.

My feet on dry ground, I moved through the rituals Kaja had taught me. Kneeling, standing, genuflecting, I offered up my mourning, my grief, all the anguish and bitter shame. I asked Glorianna to intervene with Her exacting sister, Danu. I'd rather have what Glorianna offered—love, beauty, peace—but I'd pledged myself to Danu and Her stern, unyielding justice.

After a while, I stopped thinking about anything, not wishes or regrets. I simply danced, improvising on Glorianna's prayers as the Chiyajuans elaborated on each other's songs, making it into something of my own as the elephants sang their morning song.

As the sun rose, pouring Her light over the river, I let it all flow away from me. Wash away downriver, like my wedding log. Emptying me out.

~ 16 ~

By the time I got back up to the house, my feet sore from dancing on the stones, my heart curiously still hollow, most everyone was sleeping. Except for Desta, who met me as if he'd been waiting for my appearance. Which perhaps he had been.

"Has Capa gotten up yet?" he asked.

I shook my head. "Is Ochieng all right?" Desta had never sought me out for conversation that I recalled.

"He's fine. Sleeping still." He said it with a slightly dismissive tone, as if Desta himself hadn't been doing the same, the last I saw him. "It's good, because I want to talk to you without him interfering."

I raised my brows, my mother's gesture, yes, but it centered me. In conversational combat, I'd been well trained and need not fear losing myself to awaken covered in blood.

"He protects you like a mother hen," Desta continued when I said nothing. "He's in love with you, you know."

"Yes, he told me as much."

"But you don't love him." Desta's face settled into cold lines. So much like Ochieng's face, but without his native ebullience, Desta looked harder overall. He nodded at me, as if I'd confirmed his sally, which I supposed I had. "You and I are alike," Desta said, not what I'd expected. "You have a coldness to you I recognize. We know the world is not some happy, sunny paradise. Has Ochieng ever told you how our father died?"

Again—not what I'd expected. Ochieng had never mentioned his father, and I'd never thought to ask. My fault, no doubt, as the burden of breaking my silence lay on me. For so long I hadn't been able to ask him questions, then when I could, it hadn't occurred to me to ask them.

"No," I replied, offering nothing more. Conversational combat isn't unlike the physical sort. When you don't know the skill or strategy of your opponent, it's best to keep your defense tight, providing no openings for them to strike.

Desta gave me a hard look. "You are cold, that you don't even care."

Deliberately I shrugged, Dasnarian style, raising one shoulder and letting it fall. Neither confirming nor denying. Which annoyed Desta further. I can't say why I baited him in this way, except that my mother had drilled this into me. When someone so clearly wants to tell you something, they always have a reason—and almost never is it to benefit you. Desta had some motivation for wanting to tell me this story, and I suspected he meant to hurt me with it. Perhaps to drive me away.

The joke would be on him in that case, as I'd likely be leaving. I should. I couldn't burden Ochieng and the D'tiembos with my curse any longer. All that remained was to find a way to do it so Ochieng wouldn't come after me. Preferably without hurting him, though I didn't see how that could be.

"He was murdered," Desta bit out. "By the Chimtoans."

Ah. This did not surprise me at all. In fact many of their arguments fell into place. "I'm very sorry to hear that," I said, with feeling. "Losing Femi in the same way must be especially painful."

"What do you know of it?" Desta fumed now, jaw clenched in anger. "You let him die. You have all this skill—you killed those warriors, both here and your people who came after you—but you held back."

Apparently I'd dropped my guard at some point, because his attack went right through me. Perhaps not a mortal wound, but one that bled and weakened me with it. I opened my mouth to explain, but found I had nothing to say. I had frozen. And this skill Desta referred to belonged to a part of me I'd rather cleave away. Ochieng understood—though how, I had no idea—but how could the rest of the family? All they knew was that I'd failed to act soon enough.

"And were you there to help us drive away the Chimtoans? No." Desta folded his arms, inquisitor and judge together. "You stayed behind. We have countless injured who might not be if you'd cared enough to fight for them."

"Ochieng asked me to stay with Capa," I explained, knowing as I said it that my mother would be shaking her head in condemnation. A weak counterstrike that only exposed that he'd hurt me.

Indeed, Desta smiled, a cruel and satisfied twist of his stern mouth. "Yes. Always protecting you. When will you step up and protect him?"

I didn't know how to answer that. I'd totally lost control of this sparring match, as if Kaja had disarmed me and chased me, smacking me with the flat of her blade, demanding to know what I planned to do next.

"Our father was murdered because he went alone to parley," Desta said. "Our mother stayed behind. They didn't agree, you see. And because he had no one to guard his flank, he was betrayed and she'll forever live with that guilt. She thinks that if she can grow this family, she can redeem herself. But even she knows that nothing can ever make up for not being there for her spouse. Simyu and I are a team." He made two fists and punched them together. "I know if I die, it's only because my wife died before me, to leave me unguarded."

It smacked too much of Dasnarian male hubris for me to hold my tongue. "You mean unless it's because you went down defending her."

My sudden riposte took him off guard, and he fumbled for a reply. I realized I hadn't paid much attention to the fierce Simyu, beyond admiring her. Why hadn't she been part of the hot pool celebration with Zalaika and her daughters? They had been so clear on including me, as a potential addition to the female clan, why not Simyu? Perhaps I could ask Thanda.

"Of course," Desta replied, but a beat too late and we both knew it.

I smiled at him, thin and feral, my mother's smile that always reminded me of the jewel-bright lizard pet I'd had, until it sliced my hand open with razor-sharp teeth. "Of course," I echoed, and started to turn away. Then, in a calculated aside, spoke over my shoulder. "Oh, and Desta? You should know there's nothing I won't do to protect Ochieng. His happiness is mine."

"What does that mean?" He demanded as I walked away.

I answered in Dasnarian, because those were the words I needed. "It means don't fuck with me and mine."

* * * *

When Ochieng awoke, hours later, I still hadn't slept—still too angry for it—but I had gone through the remains of my things. My side of the house had been the section that burned, though my room remained mostly intact, being on a lower level. The attackers had shot flaming arrows into the upper tiers, so the flames had spread down from there, going to the side as the breeze blew them. Some living sparks had burnt holes in my curtains and blankets, and everything lay under a coat of ash and stunk of smoke while being soaking wet from the water poured on to stop the fire.

Some part of me was grimly amused at my irritation that everything would be damp and dirty again. A small thing in the face of it all. Though

I knew Thanda, at least, shared my gallows humor, because she'd remarked that thankfully the rooms that had burned were all ones that hadn't been cleaned yet. First room and the surrounding core of the house remained intact, a small core of peace and continuity amidst the chaos and grieving.

I bagged up what could be saved. All of it fit into my travel bags again, which seemed to be a sign—if not from Danu, then of simple practicality—that I could easily remove myself from this place and move on. My sword... I didn't draw it, but I held the sheath across my palms, testing its familiar weight and balance. In a way I missed wearing it. If I had been wearing it, would the day before have gone differently? Maybe it would have been worse. With the reach and momentum of the sword, I might've killed Ochieng before he could get close enough to stay my hand and talk me out of whatever fury had seized me.

A cold shudder ran through me. Nothing Desta could say to me would make me risk coming back to my senses to find Ochieng dead by my hand. He'd called me cold and I could accept that as truth. I was my mother's daughter, after all, and a colder woman I'd never met. Regardless of what it said about me, I'd trade all the D'ticmbos to keep Ochieng safe and alive. That meant from myself as well.

Resolved, I thrust the sheathed sword, belt, and all my wrapped knives into the carry bags. They commingled there with Rodolf's manacles and cursed diamond, which seemed appropriate also. My baggage of pain.

"You shouldn't linger in here," Ochieng said from the doorway, startling me. He smiled when I turned, looking less exhausted, but his eyes still dark with weariness. "The supports might not be strong enough," he added.

"I know. Thanda says she'll find another place for me. There's a lot of reshuffling to be done." And nothing would happen until we laid Femi to rest.

"I think I can help with that. I'll carry those." He took my bags from me, shouldering them easily. I still equated size with power, so it took me aback when Ochieng's lean body demonstrated such easy strength.

I followed him down to the terrace, wondering where he planned to store my things. He kept going, up into the unburned side of the house, and into a wing I hadn't explored. Not that I'd gone into many of the parts of the house that belonged to the various subfamily groups. Part of the courtesy of affording privacy where there were no walls or doors to speak of meant not going where you weren't invited.

Ochieng climbed a set of circular stairs and emerged through the floor of a wide room actually planked in wood. The curtains were tied back on three sides, the fourth wall a smooth indentation in the granite bluff itself. Small alcoves had been carved into the rock, and various curios sat in them, glittering as the late-morning light caught them. Like most rooms in the house, this one looked out over the river, but unlike any others I'd seen, this one had that wood flooring that extended beyond the four poles of the room. A couple of chairs—made of wood frames with thick cloth slung inside like a short hammock—lounged there, overlooking the river.

And the terrace. I understood then how Ochieng had so often observed me without my knowing. I also understood this was his room.

He'd set my bags down next to a hammered metal trunk and watched me. I wouldn't have called his expression wary, but his pleasant smile covered his readiness to argue with me. Not unlike Desta that way.

"Are you keeping my things for me until Thanda can find me a new place?" I asked, offering him the out.

He sat on the trunk and stretched out his long legs, gaze traveling the area. "It's a big room."

"I see that."

"Everyone will be packing in together for a while," he pointed out, as if he were just now thinking through a problem I knew full well he'd already decided on a solution for. "Either you will have to move in with one of the other families, which means some of them will have to move in with me—or *you* could simply move in with me and save all that rearranging. A much simpler solution. Even elegant." He gave me a hopeful smile.

"You want me to … sleep, in here, with you, at the same time," I clarified, feeling foolish as I said it.

He cocked his head, a true hint of mirth sparkling in his eyes. "Well, I suppose we could take it in shifts. Like on the road, one of us standing watch while the other sleeps."

"That's not what I meant and I believe you know that."

With a resigned sigh, he opened his arms to gesture to the room. "Yes, I want you—my intended wife—to sleep in my room and in my bed, with me, at the same time. If you prefer, I can make a separate pallet to sleep on and you can have the bed. Or we can share the bed, but roll up blankets to make a wall between us. Still, I'd like to point out two things at this fork in the road. One, I've already promised—and I think repeatedly demonstrated—that I will never touch you in a way you don't fully desire, and second, if things had proceeded as planned, we'd have been sharing a room and a bed in a few days regardless."

"In a new room, with the wedding poles and all."

He shook his head slightly, then shrugged. "All along I'd hoped we could simply replace the poles in this room with those, to satisfy tradition, but this is a good space. Unless you don't like it?"

"It's lovely, but we're not married."

"You said that being engaged to marry and being married were tantamount to the same thing in your mind."

"And *you* promised that they weren't. What will everyone think of us sharing a room, a bed, when we're not married? There are names for such women in Dasnaria."

His dark eyes studied me, piercing in their perception. "Not here. Because we only conduct weddings once a year at the festival, people frequently cohabit. The formalities of marriage are only details."

"Details?" I practically gasped the word. Of course he, a man of this casual culture would see it that way. "In Dasnaria, you would be executed for even being alone with me like this. Tortured for having kissed me."

He made a dismissive sound. "And you would be still married to an abusive monster. Isn't all of this why you are no longer in Dasnaria?"

~ 17 ~

I couldn't think. Restless—and, yes, giving into my curiosity—I prowled over to the rock wall, examining the small works of art Ochieng had clearly collected in his many travels. Despite the esoteric variety of the collection, they all seemed distinctly *him* in a way I don't know that I could have articulated. A metallic fish with inlaid scales. What looked like a golden statue of a warrior. A miniature painting of a sailing ship. A painted wooden doll caught my eye, the woman's face somehow compelling, and I tucked my hands behind my back to resist the urge to touch it.

"Ah, I've been meaning to show you that," Ochieng said, coming up next to me. He plucked it from its little shelf and handed it to me. "Go ahead and open it."

"Open it?" I echoed, puzzled, examining it more closely. The doll looked like a Chiyajuan woman, with gleaming dark skin and braided hair woven with gold, her black eyes sparkling with laughter, all painted so realistically I expected to hear her sing. Her long fingers clasped over an obviously pregnant belly, her breasts and thighs full. She was naked and I blushed that Ochieng should have such a thing.

"Like so." He took it from me, his long, clever fingers sliding over the woman's body with a delicate care that sent a wave of warmth through me. Ridiculous. It must be that I was alone with him, which made no sense, as I'd been alone with him many times—so he had a point that I was being illogical about applying Dasnarian laws. Perhaps it was being alone with him in his bedchamber. *No, don't think about that.* The memories rose up, harsh, bitter, tinged with pain and humiliation. Rodolf's bedchamber, the place of nightmares. I swallowed my gorge and the horrors that wanted to rise up. Not the same. This room didn't even have bedposts and rings for chaining me. Nothing like the other. I made myself focus on Ochieng's hands, his calm words.

He'd twisted at the woman's midsection, making it seem as if her belly split open, and the two halves came apart. Inside lay another woman, similar, but with a different face, younger and less obviously pregnant.

"Ivariel?"

Ochieng said my name as if he'd said it several times already. "Yes?"

"All you all right?"

I met his gaze, willing myself to look calm, and not like a crazy woman who couldn't stand in her betrothed's bedchamber without falling into a waking nightmare. "I'm fine. Interested in the doll."

He clearly didn't believe me, but he gave me a gentle smile. "Then take the one inside."

I plucked the doll out of the bottom half-shell of the mother, aware that he'd said that to me already, also. "Sorry."

"Don't apologize," he said, a bit too sharply. Not as serene as he seemed. I raised a brow at him and his smile turned rueful. "I mean, don't be sorry for how you feel. We're all suffering in our own ways. Everyone has to find their own way through. It's not something you have to apologize for."

I wasn't so sure about that. "Does this one open, too?"

"Yes—in the same way."

Feeling for the fine line that separated the two perfectly fitted halves, I twisted as he had. They came apart easily, revealing an even younger woman within. Ochieng had fitted the first woman together and set her back on the shelf. Now he plucked the woman from inside the pieces I held, waiting for me to fit my two halves back together and place her next to her mother. I opened the new one, finding an adolescent young woman within, and inside of her, a little girl. At last, within the little girl was an infant, a small egg of a being, wrapped in colorful blankets.

Her eyes, though, were the same as the oldest mother. The same, I realized, looking at the row of them, in all the women. Bright and sparkling, laughing in delight. Carefully I set the infant at the end, the bottom sanded flat so she could stand like the others.

"Are they all the same person?" I asked.

Ochieng studied them with me. "Some say yes. Some say they are grandmothers, mothers, and daughters. What do you think?"

"You told me about this sort of doll before, when you described this house to me, with first room at the center and the layers built around that."

He smiled, and touched my cheek, fleetingly, withdrawing his hand as if uncertain if the gesture had been welcome. "You always listen. That is a thing I love about you, I should tell you. Not many people truly listen when I talk."

"That's because you talk so very much," I teased.

He mock frowned at me. "I see my mother has influenced you. But truly—you are unusual. Most people are thinking about what they want to say next, instead of truly listening."

"I don't always listen," I felt I had to say. "Sometimes I... fade out."

Sobering, he nodded, watching me closely. "I know. That's why I call you back. I don't mind because when you go inside, it's for different reasons. Will you tell me what you were thinking of, when you faded out just now?"

No. Never that. I'd told him some things, but not ... all of that. "I think the dolls are the same person," I decided, looking at them so I didn't have to face him, though I felt his discerning gaze on the side of my face like a candle flame. "Our different phases of life."

"And which is you?" he asked, allowing me that room to change the subject. Though I thought we both knew it was all one conversation.

I reached for the adolescent girl, her smile so hopeful—then realized I hadn't been her for a long time. Instead I pointed to the next oldest, the young woman, her face more mature, her eyes somehow knowing. "Probably her."

"Though, by your definition—you are all of them—just at different times."

I cast a sideways glance at him. He returned the look blandly, but I knew him too well. Deliberately I plucked up the adolescent and handed her to him. "If this doll were me, this one would be a monster." The crazed serpent inside me stirred, her scales hissing as they slid against each other.

He cupped her in his palms, cradling her with tenderness. "Or perhaps simply scarred."

"Red demon eyes," I countered. "Venomous fangs. Curved talons dripping the blood of innocents."

Lifting his gaze, he narrowed his eyes at me. "Defending innocents, and herself, from the enemy."

Slowly, I shook my head. "She's not that mindful. Her blade cuts down everyone in her path."

"You didn't attack me. Or Capa."

"Only because you stopped me."

"No," he said, surprised. "You stopped yourself. I should have told you. Once the attackers were all dead, you simply... froze. You didn't seem to know what to do next, so I called you back."

"You held my knife hand by the wrist," I reminded him.

He smiled, that rueful twist. "I promised I wouldn't let you hurt me. I was being careful."

"Wise," I told him.

A silence fell between us. And then he lifted the doll to his mouth, kissing her reverently, eyes on me all the while, and setting her on the shelf, somewhat forward of the others. A position of honor she didn't deserve.

"I'll put them back together," I said, reaching for the youngest two, but he stayed my hand, lacing his fingers with mine.

"Let's leave them unpacked for a while," he said, "I like seeing all of them. They are each beautiful in their own way. As are you. All of you." He lifted my hand to his mouth, kissing it as he had the doll. A shiver of heat ran through me and he murmured something that sounded like agreement. Turning my hand over, he smoothed open my fingers, placing kisses on the tip of each as he did, then pressing another kiss in the palm of my hand. My breath shortened, my body responding, wanting more. Wanting his mouth on me in other places, that same stirring tenderness. My skin seemed to throb with the need, starved for it. Craving the sweetness he brought.

I wished it could be like this. That I could be with him, be a wife to him and have it be only this sweet tenderness and none of the rest of it. Zalaika had been proven dramatically correct in at least that life is short, and things could change in a moment. If I'd lost Ochieng on the beach the day before, I wouldn't have had even this moment.

"It can be only this," he replied, confusing me, because I hadn't thought I'd spoken that aloud. "I promise that."

"What of your… needs?" I asked, breathless with my own needing, as I'd never truly experienced it before.

He looked up at me, mouth quirked in amusement. "I am a grown man. I've been able to handle my 'needs' for many years without a wife to see to them."

"With other women?" I asked, tugging my hand from his grasp, unreasonably jealous, as no Dasnarian woman should be. Men needed to indulge in many women, that was the way of things. Even married men seldom confined themselves to one wife. Still, the thought of Ochieng going to other women annoyed me far more than it ought. Perhaps that was me being a princess. Precious pearl. Thinking myself so special. "Never mind—I didn't mean to ask that."

"Why not? It's a perfectly reasonable question. Although it irritates me that you think I would want anyone else when I'm in love with you. I didn't ask you to marry me so I could dally with other women."

Hmm. Though I still wasn't at all sure why he did want to marry me. "Young boys then?" I asked. I'd heard plenty of tales of that sort, that young boys served in place of a female, when there were none to be had.

Ochieng looked truly horrified—and angry. "You think I would do that to a child?"

I lifted my shoulder and let it fall, starting to turn away.

But he took me by the shoulders and turned me back to face him. "No, don't do that. Some men prefer the company of other men, it's true, though I am not one of those. But to harm a child is anathema. What was done to you is anathema too. I am not that person."

I bit my lip, unwilling to cry. It seemed I wouldn't, but I was too full of too many emotions to speak. "You say it would be different between us, but how? It's too bad that kisses on my hands won't give us children."

He searched my face, a half-smile on his mouth, a frown line between his brows. "I'm not quite sure how to answer that. I feel like you have the experience to know the mechanics, but…" he trailed off, seeming uncertain how to finish that thought without upsetting me.

It made me want to laugh, that particular delicacy, so I did, laughter feeling like another sweet release—which only made him frown more deeply. Cupping his dear face in my palms, I kissed him lightly. "I think I know far more than you realize. In the seraglio we learned all sorts of ways of pleasing a man."

"But you had no men?" He asked, clearly confused.

"In theory. And we practiced on simulacrums."

He searched my face, looking for the joke.

"In fact," I continued, finding that I was enjoying myself, "perhaps I could do that for you. Would you like that?"

"What about us not being married yet?" He was hedging, because I'd seen the fire light in his eyes, the way his fingers flexed despite himself. Oh, yes—he wanted that all right.

I shrugged that off. Then reconsidered. Maybe not being married made it easier. Less like what I'd gone through before. Or, rather, what Jenna went through. Ivariel had never pledged her name to a man, only to a goddess. "You say that doesn't matter here. This would be a good test for me. If I can satisfy your needs without worrying about giving you my body, I'd rest easier about going into marriage with you."

His face was a study in conflicting emotions. Aroused and interested, yes, as any man should be by such an offer. Also bemused, a bit startled by my frankness. And torn, concern and consternation warring with the rest. "Ivariel, I…" He trailed off helplessly. "I don't know where to start here."

"I want to try this," I said firmly. Stepping away from him, I checked that all the curtains had been tied. I felt wild and a little reckless. So much sorrow and death—at least I could give him this delight, something he obviously craved and would never ask of me. I could use the skills I'd learned so painstakingly, but never truly practiced. Rodolf had wanted only my pain and submission. But I wouldn't think of that. I peered into the well of the spiral staircase. "Will anyone intrude?"

Giving me an odd look, Ochieng picked up a circular slab of wood that matched the flooring, sliding it over the gap. "Now they won't. But I still think we should—"

"Shh. Enough talking." I sounded imperious, I knew, but that helped. It made me feel more like who I'd been before Rodolf broke me. "After all, how many men can brag of being pleasured by an Imperial Princess?"

He smiled, but frowned, too. "You know that's not what this is about for me."

"I know. That's my pride speaking. You may not know it, but I have a great deal of pride."

Now he laughed. "I may have guessed that." He stilled as I approached him again, watching me almost warily, but with gratifying hunger, too, as I unlaced his shirt, pushing it off his shoulders so it fell to the floor and caressing his skin as I did. "What are the rules?" he whispered. When I raised my brows in inquiry, he shook his head, as if to clear it. "This is in your hands. I need to know what I can and can't do."

A powerful feeling, to have such an offer. "If you would…promise not to touch me?"

He nodded. "Of course."

I wanted to ask him not to chain me or hurt me, but I knew he'd be insulted by that, and I figured that fell under him not touching me.

"Anything else?" he asked, reading into my hesitation.

"The rest… can I tell you as I go along?"

"All right. I know enough now. And I'll add one—you stop the moment any of it bothers you. At all, in any way, even a little bit."

"All right."

"I mean it." He dipped his chin, catching my eye in lieu of stopping my hands. "No pushing through out of misplaced pride."

I splayed my hands over his muscled chest, the tightly curled black hairs fascinating in their texture and patterns, my fingers so pale in contrast. Looking up at him through my lashes, as I'd been taught, I gave him my most sensuous smile, touching my lower lip with the tip of my tongue. His dark eyes fired and he trembled under my hands. Excellent.

"Too much talking," I murmured. "Let me do this."

He didn't exactly agree, but as I pressed a kiss to that enticing hollow between his collar bones, he made a helpless sound of lust that was exactly perfect.

~ 18 ~

I explored his naked chest with my hands, following with my mouth, teasing those spots said to be sensitive, experimenting with kisses, licks, light sucking, and bites, both soft and sharp, finding which he preferred. He shivered under it all, giving me a heady sense of power. It also gave me pleasure, which I hadn't at all expected. Without even touching me, by giving himself over like this, Ochieng had aroused me, too. My sex ached and grew slick as it never had for my late husband. Much as it had angered him at the time, in retrospect I took a savage satisfaction in it.

Everything about me had angered him and none of it had anything to do with who I really was. He'd been able to command my obedience, but not my genuine feelings and responses. Something of a revelation. But I wouldn't think about that now. This moment should be about me and Ochieng only, together.

Ochieng moaned under my ministrations, and when I looked up, I saw he had his head tipped back, throat tense and straining, hands clenched in fists at his sides. Doing his best by me, keeping to the promise not to touch me, though he clearly wanted to.

His cock thrust against his loose trousers, moisture leaking from the tip soaking through the cloth. I took him in my hand, a bit startled by his length and girth there. Definitely nothing like my late husband's withered member that had stayed flaccid until the sight of my blood and the sound of my screams awakened it. *Don't think about it.*

I squeezed, finding the right pressure, and Ochieng made a choking sound. Oh yes, just like that. I stroked him, and his hips rode towards me as I pulled, and he swallowed convulsively. I'd best move this along, if I wanted to try everything I had in mind. But I needed to alter our positions, to make sure I didn't succumb to the bad memories.

"Do you mind lying down, on the bed maybe?" I asked.

He cracked his eyes open. They were unfocused, not quite following.

"I think I'd rather not kneel," I explained. That might be too much as it had been with Rodolf. "If you could lie down then I'll be able to continue."

"Ivariel." His eyes cleared and he tried to pull back, but I didn't release him and he halted, hands dancing around mine as if he'd like to pull them off, but mindful of his promise not to touch me. With a sound of frustration he raked his fingers into his hair, pressing the heels of his hands to his temples and squeezing his eyes closed.

"You don't have to do this," he got out.

"I want to. Is it a problem for you to lie down? On your back," I clarified.

He choked out a laugh. "No. No, it's not a problem. If you're sure."

"I'm sure."

"You'll have to let me go." He grinned abruptly and raised a brow at me. "Unless you want to walk me over there."

I laughed, too, surprising myself. I hadn't known there could be laughter during sex. Letting him go, I dipped a curtsy, full formal court style. "As you will, sir."

He walked over to his pallet and lowered himself to it. "Keep my pants on?"

"For now, yes." I liked being the one to decide these things. "But... Ochieng?"

He froze. "Problem?"

"No, no. Not that." I folded my hands together, unsure if he'd mind the request.

"Ask, Ivariel," he said gravely, his tone gentle, gaze warm.

"Would you take your hair out of the queue? I'd like to see it loose."

I'd surprised him. "Of course. You could have taken the tie out yourself." He snagged the tie and yanked it out, his hair falling around his face.

I came over and straddled his legs, kneeling on either side of his thighs, widely enough that I didn't touch him, and slipped my hands into his hair, savoring the soft, silken texture. He'd closed his eyes, holding still for me. "Is this all right?" I asked.

He opened his eyes, looking at me with amusement. "You've had your hands in more intimate places than that."

"Yes, but I wasn't sure... Dasnarian men wear their hair very short." My fingers caught a little, dragging in his hair, and he let his head fall back, eyes drifting closed again. "I didn't know what the rules were for it."

"No rules," he murmured. "Only what pleases you."

"That's a gift to me," I told him, feeling a little shy to say so. "To be able to do what pleases me."

He opened his eyes, gazing into mine, so full of feeling that my heart seemed to swell, as if it might overfill and break. "If you'll let me," he said, "I'll spend the rest of my life letting you do what pleases you."

"But why?" I whispered.

"Because I love you," he replied, as if that were the obvious answer. And to him it was.

I leaned in and kissed him, holding him with my hands sunk in his hair, and he returned it, following my lead. When I parted my lips, so did he. When I touched my tongue to his, a shockingly intimate contact, he returned the caress in kind. I explored his mouth as I had his chest, finding what he liked, what burned into his control, the spots that made him tremble.

He leaned back on his arms still but they weakened as I teased him into a state of near delirium, his breath coming in harsh pants. Taking the kisses to his face, I rained them on him. Rose-petal kisses, we call them, and I showered them on his upturned face like a benediction, soothing him.

"Lie back," I murmured, and he let out a grateful sigh, at last giving way and falling back with a sound of relief. Following him down, I took the kisses to the sharp line of his jaw, and the tender skin beneath. Then up to his ear, tracing the elegant inner folds with my tongue, sucking, then nipping at the lobe, making him groan and clench his fists in the blankets.

My teachers would be proud, I thought, as I tried the tricks they'd taught me—and improvised from there. They'd said that each man is different, that learning to play his body is an art, like learning a new dance. He is the music you dance to, but your steps set the cadence and harmony. I finally understood that now, strumming the fine instrument of my lover. The first true lover I'd ever had.

Following the lines of his body down, I built the tension of the song we played together. The scent of his body, the quake of a muscle, the harsh groan and tender sigh, all guiding me to give him the utmost pleasure. All the world fell away until I knew only him, only the taste of his skin against my tongue, the silken feel of him under my hands, the expanse of his body on display for my savoring, the sounds he made all the music I needed.

When I reached his groin, he made a strange, choked sound—almost of despair, and I paused in undoing the laces of his pants. He had his hands over his face, knuckles white from tension.

"Is this all right?" I asked him.

He laughed, a hoarse sound, creaking, with a desperate edge. "Just tell them I died happy," he grated out.

I paused, he sounded so pained. "Should I stop?"

His jaw flexed, and he swallowed, hard. "Do you want to?"

Such a lovely man. He'd let me, if I said I did. Tempting to toy with him, but that trust between us seemed too fragile still to test with teasing. "Lift your hips," I told him, and he did without question. I slid the pants off him, tossing them aside, taking the time to enjoy the bounty of his masculine beauty.

Sometime I'd love to start at his feet, kissing the toes, the erogenous point at the arch, behind the ankle, that lighter skin between his toes. But not today. His whole body strained with the effort to stay still for this, his cock rising and falling of its own accord, as if reaching for my touch.

So I crawled back up his body, indulging in tracing the lines of the muscles in his legs, the silky texture of the soft skin of his inner thighs. I nuzzled my cheek against his groin, the scent of him sharper there, making me want to take him into me. A startling thought—especially that it didn't make me feel ill.

Delicately I touched his shaft with my tongue, intending to trace the lines there, too, but he nearly convulsed, a strangled cry escaping him.

"Ochieng?" I asked.

"Just..." He was panting. "For the love of your goddess, Ivariel, I can't hold back any more. I … just can't."

I smiled, well pleased with myself. There would be other days to extend his tolerance, to take him close to the edge, and pull back. Other days. I'd been able to do this, and I'd be able to do it again. I looked forward to it.

"Ivariel?" he asked, lifting his head to look at me.

"I'm here. Watch." Taking his shaft firmly at the root, I swallowed him into my mouth, loving the way he cried out, throwing his head back and arching helplessly as he orgasmed. He filled my mouth with his seed and I swallowed it gladly, wishing only I could send it to my eggs, that we could make a baby this way.

I controlled the final climax of our pairing, milking him, guiding him back from the agonizing peak of pleasure with all the gentleness I could muster. Here the untutored can fail to take care of their partner, letting him drop back to earth without the silken grace of female comfort to soften his descent. I learned him, still finding what soothed, when to stop touching the overworked sweet spots, transferring my attention to a gentle massage of smoothing caresses.

Making my way back up his body, I placed a kiss on his forehead, a final token of the delights I wished for him. He smiled, barely, a slight curve of his generous mouth, eyes closed, arms and hands at last relaxed at his sides, his body long and lax with release. Many men fell asleep at this point, I understood, so I waited quietly, so as not to disturb him. And also not quite sure what else to do. My lessons had never detailed past that. I supposed because the man would've known. He'd either summon an escort for me back to the seraglio or inform me of the next desired service.

After only a moment, Ochieng rolled his head toward me, opening his eyes. He lifted a hand, offering it. "Will you lie beside me?" He asked, voice somehow both rough and sweet.

I considered it, testing myself for a reaction, like rolling a new food in my mouth to check if I liked it enough to swallow. It seemed to be all right. So I eased down beside him, and he wrapped the extended arm around me, snuggling me against his side. Comforting, and yet loosely enough that I didn't feel trapped. How well he understood me.

"How are you?" he asked, sounding careful.

"I feel good," I replied immediately. "Though I have many techniques yet to try. I only got to a few."

He chuckled, then cleared his throat. "I'm not sure if I'm intrigued or terrified."

I looked down at his body, his lax cock filling and straightening again. "I believe you overstate your fear." I trailed a finger down his flat belly, intent on renewing my attentions to him, but he stopped me. A gentle touch, then laced his fingers with mine and drew our joined hands up between us, turning on his side as he did to face me. "Am I wrong?" I asked, made uncertain by his serious expression.

But he smiled, a soft and tender curve. "No. I shall never again scoff at my Imperial Princess, or her tenacity, patience, and cruel ability to tease a man past all sanity."

"Then what?" I searched his face. Something that I hadn't done correctly. I hadn't meant to be cruel. "Didn't I please you?"

He sobered, eyes filling with some emotion I didn't recognize. He brought our joined hands to his mouth, kissing the back of mine. "Oh, Ivariel. You are as exquisitely talented in this as you are in all things. But I don't want you to pleasure me. No, no—don't look at me like that. I don't mean not at all, or not ever, but I want us to share these things. What you did for me was incredible. Can't you see I want to give that to you, too?"

I eyed him, feeling hesitant. "I don't know that part."

"What do you mean?"

Restless, I shifted, but he kept ahold of me. Not tightly, but enough that I'd have to tear away. I didn't really want to. Lying beside him felt good. Like leaning against Efe or Violet. Safe and ... loved? Was that the name to put to this feeling?

"Ivariel, talk to me," he reminded me.

"I mean that, I learned to please a man, but all I know about ... the rest is—" I broke off, the sick rising.

"Is what?"

I shrugged, then pulled our hands apart, needing to sit up and catch my breath. "Submit. Give over my body. And, Ochieng, I'm sorry, but I just don't think I can—"

"La." He'd sat up, too, putting gentle hands on my shoulders, bracing me against the tremors that had seized me. "Relax. Let it go. I'm the one who's sorry."

"All right." I drew in a ragged breath. "We won't speak of it."

"Not at the moment," he agreed, though I didn't miss the caveat.

"We meant to go dig out Efe," I said. "And we should check on Capa."

"Let's do that then."

I stood and retrieved his clothes, handing them over, wondering if I should help but he didn't seem to expect it.

"Ivariel?" He asked from the wash basin.

"Yes?" I braced myself, for whatever of a hundred questions he could ask. I would have to tell him at some point, what it had been like between me and Rodolf. So he'd know. It wasn't fair that he didn't know.

"Will you share this room and my bed with me?" He wiped his face with a cloth, giving me a hopeful look.

I had to laugh, having nearly forgotten how all of this had started. "I will, Ochieng. If only because I don't wish to sleep on the beach."

~ 19 ~

We slid aside the cover from the hole to the stairwell, and I commented about how Ochieng's room had so much wood when very little of the rest of the house did.

"I've been a bachelor for many years," he replied. "And it saddened me at times, to be around my siblings' families, especially stuck here in the rainy season. So I began finding ways to plane and fit together small pieces of wood. I made this floor over many years."

We'd descended back into the lower levels, the house full of the sounds of sleep or mourning, like sinking into a pool of sorrow I'd managed to forget for a blissful space of time. Glancing at Ochieng, I saw he felt it, too, so I took his hand, lacing his fingers with mine, in the way he'd taught me. It seemed wrong that we'd taken some happiness—like stealing a snack while everyone else starved—and yet the smile he gave me made it hard to regret that.

Upon reflection, it seemed much of life since leaving the seraglio had been like that. Before I left seemed a long blur of sameness—the tropical warmth, being bathed and groomed, dancing, lounging, decorating myself with the finest jewels of the empire. There'd been a perfection to it, but nothing stood out, other than the punishments I'd rather forget, and which I'd quickly learned to avoid by being exquisitely obedient.

Since then, however, the sweet memories stood out in high relief, vividly colored in my mind. Standing on the deck of the *Valeria*, watching the enormous whales move beneath the crystalline water. The moment Kaja gave me my sword. Eating in that outdoor café in Ehas, drinking wine and savoring my freedom. Lying in the dark on the deck of the *Robin*, listening to Ochieng spin tales from the patterns in the stars. Seeing elephants for the first time. Ochieng kissing me while the pre-rains light melted golden thick around us. These had become my new jewels, shining and precious, and ones that I'd keep forever in a special place in my heart and mind.

Now I added this new one, the sweet memory of tasting Ochieng's body in the quiet intimacy of his room, drowning my senses in him. I'd remember it for the rest of my life, no matter what came next.

It seemed that the good moments became all that much better for standing out from the struggle. I didn't understand what that meant, but maybe I didn't need to yet. Somehow, though, I thought Kaja might have understood this. Perhaps Danu teaches it. It seemed Her stern sword and unflinching justice would be balanced by these shining soft moments of sheer happiness.

We stayed quiet until we got outside, going down the steps through the storehouse. "Why did you stay a bachelor all those years?" I asked when we no longer risked disturbing anyone. "If it saddened you not to have a family of your own, why didn't you marry?"

"Because you weren't here yet," he replied easily. His smile widened at whatever he saw in my face. "Argue the point with me all you like, lovely Ivariel, but I knew I needed to wait for someone special. No matter how long she dragged her feet in finding me."

I made a dismissive sound.

"It's true. If only because I knew I needed a wife who wouldn't pitch me off the terrace when I told her one too many stories during the rainy season," he added, sliding me a grin.

"Don't be so sure I won't!" I told him, then closed my mouth over the astonishment. Who was I that I could say such a thing to a man? But he only laughed.

"See? This is true. And why you are the perfect woman for me. Absolutely worth waiting for."

I didn't reply to that, still not sure how long this moment of happiness could last. Once I'd believed in forever—until "forever" had become a death sentence. If I'd learned nothing else in this last year, I'd at least learned to always look past the surface, especially an enticing one. Pretty things looked that way to cover the ugliness beneath. That included myself.

By mutual accord, we took the path around to the beach to check on Capa first. Along the way, we passed various men and women of the family, hired workers, even some from town—all standing guard at various points. Mostly watching the approaches from downriver. They nodded to us in silence, all song banished. I hated everything about that. Too much like the Imperial Palace, with the guards watching everything, all the time.

But I didn't say so. Instead I told Ochieng about the elephants at dawn. How they'd sung and I'd danced. He commented that he was sorry to have missed it, and I could tell he meant it, a bruised regret settling around him.

Capa hadn't moved, opening one weary eye to see that it was us, then closing it again with a sigh that billowed out of her. Violet still stood with her, as did a number of other elephants. Several human guards had been posted to the beach, and for once I didn't mind Desta's militant zeal. Ochieng checked Capa's wounds, while I stood by and fretted. Violet dusted me with her trunk and I leaned on her, sharing our mutual worry.

Ochieng hadn't said anything about me taking up my sword or daggers, though he had to know they were in the bags he'd carried to his rooms in his preemptive effort to ensure my moving in with him. I'd stuffed the blade I'd taken from Ayela in there, too. Seeing all the weapons around me made my palms itch to check mine, a habit I'd finally taken as my own from Kaja's determined training. The gauzy dress felt wrong, also, and it occurred to me that I should've donned my fighting leathers.

But I hadn't worn them since that night. Desta's accusing glare hovered in my mind. *He's always protecting you. When will you step up and protect him?* Ochieng didn't need protecting though—and if he did, likely he needed protecting from me, the greatest threat to his enduring happiness and peace of mind.

I should leave now. The time was right. I'd given Ochieng a gift of pleasure to repay all he'd given me, at least in part, and added a jewel of a memory to my small hoard. I couldn't help the D'tiembos or Nyambura, not when I couldn't control the monster within. For a while there, I'd had a glimpse of the future that I could live in that room with Ochieng. Now that possibility had become equally impossible, and I didn't understand who I'd been in that moment that I'd even entertained the notion.

I was broken, and I would never heal. I would not allow myself to close my eyes to that stark truth again.

Ochieng approached me, expression grave. "It doesn't look good. We can't hope for much."

"No," I replied. "But we've known that all along."

He cocked his head ever so slightly. "You've been sure Capa wouldn't survive?"

Capa. Not me. I'd fallen into my usual self-absorption. "She lost so much blood," I offered, hoping to cover my true thoughts.

"That's true." He sighed. "Let's go see what we can do for Efe. I'd hoped to ask Violet for help, but I hate to make her leave Capa."

As we'd talked, Violet had returned to her fallen sister, standing guard over her, their trunks intertwined as if they held hands.

"It wouldn't be fair to either of them. Maybe Efe will be hungry."

We detoured back to the storehouse, filling a woven grass basket with all of Efe's favorite treats. Passing the training grounds, I saw Desta and Simyu, among others, drilling with some of the other elephants. They wore elaborate harnesses, with shields strapped over their vulnerable spots. The riders brandished long spears or shot arrows from their backs as the elephants ran at surprisingly nimble speeds. Nothing like a horse, and with none of that grace, but something about the elephants' size gave their riders extra strength, and they easily struck down human-shaped targets.

A vision of Zalaika flashed against my mind's eye, her hair in long, streaming braids, her profile sharp and gilded with fire as she clung to Bimyr's side, her machete slicing through Dasnarian armor as easily as she sliced fruit for her family. Zalaika who hadn't gone with her husband into danger.

"I'm sorry I never asked about your father, how he died," I said. Then realized how abrupt the introduction of that topic sounded.

Ochieng, however, never bothered by the labyrinthine turn of my thoughts, glanced at me. "Desta told you?"

"How did you know?"

Ochieng looked off into the distance, a sad and thoughtful expression on his face. "Desta... dwells. Broods. It may not be fair of me, but I think it's not healthy. Our father is gone. This attack brought that forward, but how it happened is no more relevant than that the sun sets." Looking back at me, he ran a hand over my hair, settling it at the back of my neck and stroking there. "Besides, it never surprised me that you didn't ask. The way you grew up, your father wasn't a part of your world."

"My father was there, in the Imperial Palace."

"Ah, but how often did you interact with him?"

I hadn't even met him before I turned eighteen and left the seraglio, though I'd been presented to him when I was born. Ochieng knew that and smiled, again a sad twist to it. "My father was a huge part of my life," he offered. "And though I miss him deeply, I think I'm most fortunate to have had him to guide me, to help me become a man. It's better to have something, to treasure time with a person, even if you must lose them, than to have them live but not be part of your life, don't you think?"

~ 20 ~

I didn't know—it seemed like I'd suffered so much loss and so little treasuring that I had no perspective on the question. So I didn't reply. And Ochieng allowed me my silence, as he always did. Besides, he'd made his point and likely knew it. He might suspect I still harbored half a plan to leave and had been speaking to those thoughts, too, with his uncanny ability to read me.

We found Efe in the thin mud of the elephants' lagoon, the only one in there. She'd backed herself into a sheltered wallow, the reeds towering around her, bright green from the rains. If I hadn't known to look for her, I'd have taken the dome of her head for a gray rock, the tip of her trunk for a bit of floating detritus.

She stirred when we called her name, lifting her head high enough to blink open her eyes, clots of mud clinging to her lavish eyelashes. Helva would've killed for such lashes, it occurred to me, and a surge of love and missing her left me breathless.

If I left, maybe I could journey back to Dasnaria after all. With Rodolf dead, I legally counted as a widow. I could disguise myself and sneak back into the Imperial Palace. I'd promised to return for my sisters, with every intention of doing so. Though when I'd made the promise I'd thought it would be a matter of traveling from within the empire, not across the greater world. And what would I do once there? I had no more power to free them now than I'd had then.

"Try tempting her with this one." Ochieng turned my hand palm up and placed Efe's favorite fruit in it, the tenor of his voice indicating he knew he drew me out of deep thought.

"Why me?" I asked reflexively, the fruit cool and fragrant in my palm. My stomach stirred and I realized I couldn't recall when I'd last eaten. "Because she likes you better." Then he grinned. "Since you're hungry, too, have a bite to entice her."

I wrinkled my nose at him, but knelt down in the mud. I'd have to wash and change clothes for the burial of Femi anyway. I'd long since learned not to expect to stay clean while working with my big friends who loved to dunk people as a sign of affection.

"Efe," I crooned, making an effort to call from my heart, too, so she'd sense my good will. "Efe, darling—look what I have for you." Taking Ochieng's suggestion, I bit into the fruit. It was a bit mealy from being stored so long, but full of juice and sunshine. I held it out on my palm toward the tip of her trunk. "Smell that? So yummy. Mmm."

Her trunk twitched, but she didn't move otherwise.

"That was a terrible effort. Don't you have experience coaxing little kids to eat?" Ochieng chided me.

"No," I snapped over my shoulder. "The servants did that."

"Such a princess."

"You're just now figuring that out?" I inched forward, waving the fruit nearer Efe's trunk. "Don't listen to mean old Ochieng, honey. I'm your sister under the skin. Us princesses have to stick together."

She lifted her head a bit, eye glimmering less balefully, her trunk gliding in my direction. "That's it. Tasty snack for you." Her trunk stopped a good arm's length from me, however. "Come a little closer and it's yours," I promised, edging a bit farther out, holding out the fruit to better entice her.

"You're going to end up in the lagoon at that rate," Ochieng observed.

"Quiet. I'm focusing. Here Efe. Look what I have for you."

Her trunk straining for me, Efe moved a little, nearly closing the distance. She reached, but couldn't quite.

"Come on, sweetheart," I crooned. "You're almost there."

She eyed me, then the fruit. Then lunged up to grab it from my hand. The sudden movement displaced the liquid mud, the semi-solid ground beneath me falling away. Sucking me right under.

I shrieked as I went—inhaling a mouthful of mud in my carelessness— and floundered in the stinking, sticky stuff. Efe's trunk wrapped around my waist and she helpfully nudged me to the surface then pushed me to the bank, making fretful noises. Ochieng grabbed my seeking hands and pulled me onto solid ground—*not* making concerned sounds but laughing his ass off.

I sat up, wiping the mud from my face so I could at least open my eyes and glare at him. He sat beside me, a wagging finger pointing at me, while he laughed so hard he gasped for breath and tears ran down his face. I batted at his finger and turned to face Efe, who stood over me, mud sheeting off of her in great glops, anxiously exploring me with her trunk.

"I'm fine, honey, I'm fine," I reassured her. At last satisfied, she cast about for the fruit, which floated nearby, happily snaking it up and eating it with relish. "No, don't—" I stopped when my caution came too late. "That thing was filthy, Efe!"

"Elephants don't care about such things," Ochieng managed. "It won't hurt her."

"Good," I retorted, "since I drank a bellyful of the stuff." I turned to spit out the mud making my teeth grind grittily against each other. How my mother would cringe to see me. The notion made me viciously happy. One day I would return and she would see the woman I'd become. And I'd enjoy every moment of it.

"I tried to warn you," Ochieng said, eyeing me.

"Ah," I said, "but you see, it was all a part of my clever plan." I gestured triumphantly to Efe, who—apparently convinced I wouldn't drown—now helped herself to the basket of fruit we'd brought, tail and ears flapping with perky interest, as if she'd never sulked at all. "Efe is out of the mud."

"True are your words," Ochieng said.

I wrinkled my nose at him. "That's not exactly a correct usage."

He took my hand, lacing our fingers together, unbothered by my filthy state. "Let's take Efe to Capa and the others, then clean off in the river."

"Is it safe?" I frowned at him.

"The current is slowing, and the elephants will watch out for us." He squeezed my hand. "I promise I won't let the river have you. You're far too precious."

"You know what your mother says. The river takes what she wishes, whether we yield it willingly or not."

His smile faded, and I was sorry to have said it.

* * * *

We gathered in the late afternoon to consign Femi to the afterlife. I hadn't ever attended any kind of memorial for the dead before, something that struck me suddenly as I did my best to ape what the others did. Fortunately Thanda had guessed that I'd at least not know Chiyajuan—or Nyamburan, I wasn't sure—customs and gave me a shapeless gray dress to wear, along with a finely woven veil of the same color to drape over my head, pins holding it to my hair. The men wore similar robes, and small rounds of the veil fabric on their heads. Seeing everyone gathered at the base of the hill, I would have called the color "elephant gray," they looked so much like a cluster of the tribe.

So perhaps the customs went even more specific, to those of the D'tiembo family, who identified with their totem elephants above all.

I stayed with the cluster of women not in Femi's direct line, which meant Thanda, Simyu, and other cousins and cousins' wives, along with some of the men. Before abandoning me to Thanda's care, Ochieng had told me he'd join me there.

Soon I saw why. Zalaika, Palesa, and Nafula soon appeared, riding Violet, Bimyr, and another elephant whose name I didn't know. But the women rode backwards, their heads and bodies entirely draped in the gray veils. Palesa and Nafula's husbands guided their elephants with a hand on their jaw, while Ochieng and Desta flanked Violet, guiding her for their mother and matriarch. They sang a song I hadn't heard before, the women keening high notes that sounded like the embodiment of the agony of grief, the men's somber voices booming below with the stepping of the elephants.

Between them, the three elephants pulled a cart, which held Femi's body on a bed of dried flower blossoms mounded on hay. Behind the cart walked all the D'tiembo children, Ayela at the fore, like a smaller procession of elephants. Their higher voices chimed in the keening, too, sending shivers through my ears.

Until then I thought that the children must have been kept away, protected from such a horrible experience, but apparently not. Following behind Thanda, I joined the rest of the family bringing up the rear of the solemn parade, which turned—not surprisingly—to the river.

We passed the guards, still on alert, none of them of the family. All saluted. Then joined in the song, picking up the refrain and passing it back. It was the first Chiyajuan song I'd heard, I realized, that didn't change as different singers picked it up. This song remained the same, frozen in place, just as Femi's young life would. I choked on that, feeling the ultimate impact of death, that the song stopped moving with it, and I couldn't have sung, even if I'd known how.

In the seraglio, no one ever died. Not even our pets, who came and went. Instead of death, we had a pleasant vanishing. I'd never seen anything dead until I killed a man. And that had seemed so unreal.

It hadn't been real to me until I walked in the funeral procession, the dirge rolling with the wheels of the cart and the solemn scuffing of the elephants. Even they seemed to understand death better than I.

For some reason I thought of the dolls, how one lay inside the other. Perhaps in the smallest one should be a gray seed of death. No—that wasn't right. It should be a gray veil, enveloping the oldest doll. In truth, the biggest and oldest doll should've been an old woman, and I didn't know why it hadn't been.

Strange, circular thoughts, stirred by the cycling dirge for a child who should've had his whole life to live.

We reached the beach, where an odd sort of raft had been drawn up on the rocks as far from Capa as possible. She still lay as she had when we brought Efe to her. And Efe still stayed with her and some of the other elephants not in the procession. She looked skittish to my eye, not at all certain why so many people were invading her beach.

Still, she stayed near Capa, stalwart at least in her determination to help her fallen sister. Efe forgot her own fears when another needed help, which I could likely learn from.

Much as I would've preferred to go be with Efe and Capa, I followed the others to the raft. They halted, the women dismounted, and then Nafula and her husband went to the cart and lifted the pallet holding Femi between them. Ochieng and Desta had helped Zalaika down, and they and Palesa and her husband now followed as Femi's parents carried him to the raft.

Zalaika seemed so old, walking with pained steps between her sons, their hands supporting her elbows, nearly staggering on the uneven stones. But when she drew near the raft holding Femi's bier, she straightened, then lifted the front of her veil, rolling it up so it caught on the pins holding it in place. The breeze off the river caught it, so it seemed to float behind her like morning mist.

Palesa and Nafula echoed the gesture, like a dance they'd long practiced together. As they turned so I caught glimpses of their faces, I nearly gasped aloud. Amidst all the soft grays, they'd painted their faces a startling crimson. Their eyes shone like dark stars in a field of freshly spilt blood.

A shiver of the numinous thrilled over my skin, like breath of fire and chill of ice at once. It was a sensation I'd associated with Danu's presence in the past—back when I'd mostly believed that Danu had accepted my vow and set Her hand on me and guided my footsteps.

Kaja's faith in Danu had been utter and absolute. She'd never doubted that Danu led her to help me—and that the warrior goddess of the bright blade and unflinching justice had taken her on her next mission. Had she doubted, when she faced death? No, I'm sure she hadn't. I could almost see Kaja grinning in my mind at the foolish thought.

It seemed she looked at me out of Zalaika's dark eyes, which had fixed on me.

"We send our child into the next world," she intoned. "Too soon. Too young. The next world has gained the brightest of spirits—and now owes us a debt. Who shall claim this debt?"

Boom boom. The drums rolled out the demand, the peoples' feet stomping with it. "We will," they averred, voices deep as the drums.

"Who shall claim this debt?" Palesa demanded, her eyes also finding me. Kaja and Danu, staring me down, expectant.

Boom boom. "We will!"

Nafula had been staring down at her dead son, but now she raised her head, staring at me, Danu in her gaze also. They were the dolls, black eyes full of rage and grief, but ranged together as on the shelf. I felt as if I'd sprung from them, wrested from inside their darkness. I realized I'd folded my hands over my belly, as if to protect the seed that had not yet been planted.

Danu's hand lay heavy on me and I realized She'd never left. The goddess had simply lightened Her demand while I healed. But I'd vowed my sword to Her and She hadn't released me from that promise. I'd thought She'd led my footsteps here as a gift.

Now I understood I'd been sent to the D'tiembos to do Danu's work, and the goddess expected me to take up my sword.

Nafula spoke clearly, if softly. Speaking directly to me. "Who will claim this debt?"

Boom. I stepped forward and the drums missed their second beat.

"I will."

~ 21 ~

"This isn't your battle," Ochieng said, yet again. He'd followed me to his—our—room, leaning against one of the four poles with his arms crossed, watching me lay out the contents of my bags on his painstakingly crafted wood floor.

"Your mother, sister, and niece spoke to me with the voice of Danu," I replied, marveling at how serene I sounded. "It is my battle. My goddess summons me."

"You told me you're a fraud. Not a true warrior priestess at all." His voice sounded tight, and I glanced up to find his face and jaw equally set.

"And you wanted me to take up my weapons again," I pointed out.

He threw up his hands, the violence of his frustration propelling him off the pole. "So you would feel more like yourself again. So you would *live* instead of drifting about like a ghost of yourself."

Unfolding my leathers and brushing them out, I considered that. Ochieng's sunniness concealed worry that he never showed outwardly. If I survived to become his wife, I'd have to learn to look for what he didn't show or say. "I owe your family a debt of life," I replied calmly.

He made a disgusted sound. "Ridiculous."

I glanced up at him again. "Your family saved my life. Do you deny I would've died out there if you all hadn't ridden to my rescue?"

He opened his mouth to retort, but for once words escaped him. I nodded. "You know it's true. Ochieng, I have been rescued three times now. First Harlan risked his life, lost his rank, and destroyed his future to help me escape. Kaja helped a strange woman, for no other reason than because it was the right thing to do. I wouldn't have survived, or at least escaped recapture, without her help. And you and your family risked yourselves and the elephants to save me from my late husband's men. That's three I owe, if not directly to your family, then to Danu."

"All of these people acted out of love for you or for their own reasons. That doesn't mean you owe anyone anything. Those actions were gifts, freely given," he bit out.

I reached into the bag, pulling out the plain wedding bracelets my late husband had forced back on me, their broken ends where Ochieng had had them cut off me ragged and sharp. The diamond ring I tucked in a pocket of my fighting leathers. The bracelets, still dangling their chains, I held up. "Do you know what these are?"

He frowned. "Of course."

"No, I mean, I want you to understand what it means that I twice had wedding bracelets locked onto my wrists—and twice someone else cut them away for me. I'm grateful for that, but I also feel I owe a debt, perhaps to Danu and Her sisters, for all the help I've received. It's time for me to help someone else. And I've been asked to do it. I cannot turn away from that call."

Ochieng was silent a moment, then came over to squat in front of me. "I thought you said you weren't even sure your goddess existed, that you didn't truly believe as an acolyte should."

I lifted a shoulder and let it fall, feeling very Dasnarian in that moment, full of fatalistic lack of expectation. If anyone can be filled with an absence, it's the Dasnarians. "Kaedrin, a Warrior Priestess of Danu who helped Kaja train me, said once that many people think they must believe in a god or goddess, and once they do, they'll follow the practice they demand. The followers of Danu believe in practice first, as the foundation. You learn the forms, you practice diligently, and uphold Danu's law. This creates the framework for faith to fill."

He regarded me thoughtfully. "I don't think I understand."

"I'm saying it doesn't matter what I believe. I need to do the work. And I haven't been. I need to act as a Warrior Priestess of Danu, which was the bargain I made with the goddess in exchange for Her protection."

"Maybe the bargain has been fulfilled," he said quietly. "She protected you and brought you here, to me, to all of this. You can't tell me you don't love it here. I can see it in you." He took my hand and lifted it, laying it on his chest over his heart, so I could feel the steady beating beneath. "This. This is real, Ivariel. Not faith, or belief, or what you think you owe."

I curled my fingers a little, sinking into the feel of him. "You call me 'Ivariel' so easily, but under this woman that you met on a sailing ship lies another. I'm still Jenna. I wasn't able to save myself, I was too late to save Femi, but I can do this. I can save others."

"What are you going to do?" He demanded, holding my hand hard against him with both of his, dark eyes as sparking fierce as the women's had been. "Will you ride off alone and demand the Chimtoans bring Femi back to life? No amount of faith can bring him back from ashes. Will you draw blood to balance our blood lost? Because that only means more people die."

We stared into each other, each trying to see into the shadows. Even now the burning raft with Femi's body floated down the river, becoming ash that would become the current that went to the great sea beyond. And the elephants stood vigil, Capa still lying half in the water, a forest of legs protecting her.

I gently withdrew my hand from under Ochieng's, took up the leather roll of daggers and unlaced it, spreading it open so their lethal edges gleamed in the lantern light. Then I set my sheathed sword beneath them. "I don't know yet. Danu will guide my feet, my hands and my sword." And maybe Kaja, who'd promised she'd act as Danu's handmaiden, keeping an eye on me. All I knew was that I had to do this—that I'd been called to—and I had to find my own way.

"And you call me impossible," he said under his breath, standing again and glaring at me with crossed arms. I didn't think I'd ever made Ochieng angry at me before and it hurt me on a strange level.

I stood to face him. "I don't know how to do this. How do people who love each other fight?"

He turned his head slightly, as if he hadn't quite heard me correctly. "What did you say?"

"I asked you how do I fight with you about this? I don't like making you angry with me, and I feel sure you won't beat me to exact my obedience, but I must do this thing that you don't want me to do, so—"

Ochieng held up a hand, stopping my explanation. Then laughed a little. "There was a time I wouldn't have predicted you could be so full of speeches. Back up. Did you say you love me?"

I paused there, considering him. "I must. I thought you knew that."

"No." He shook his head slowly. "You've never told me so. I'd remember."

"I showed you, earlier today. When I pleasured you, as I've never done for anyone. You said I don't know how to recognize love, so I could be wrong, but… it hurts me when you're hurt, and it bothers me greatly that you're angry with me. And even through all of that I still want to touch you and have you touch me so…" I lifted a shoulder and let it fall.

"It's traditional," he said, a line between his brows as he searched my face, "to make something of a declaration of it, not to assume the other knows."

"You told me you loved me while standing in waist-deep flood waters holding onto a crazy elephant's child," I pointed out.

His frown cleared and he grinned abruptly. "True are your words. It appears you and I are quite non-traditional." Then he uncrossed his arms and held out his hands. I took them, and he drew me closer, which felt much nicer than him glaring at me. "My Ivariel—do you really love me?"

"I agreed to marry you, didn't I?"

He quirked a brow. "Given your history, that's not a definite correlation."

I had to laugh, surprising myself that laughter and my former marriage could occupy the same space in my mind. "True are your words," I returned. "But yes, if love is what I think it is, then I do love you. And Efe, and Violet and Capa. Probably Ayela, too."

He laughed, shaking his head at me. "At least you put me at the top of the list."

"I told you I don't know how to do these things."

Tugging me closer, testing for my hesitation and finding none, Ochieng pulled me into his arms, cupping my head so we were cheek to cheek, his breath in my ear. "I love you beyond all imagining," he whispered. "I couldn't bear to lose you."

I turned my head and kissed his ear, tracing the sensitive part of the elegant shell of it that I'd found aroused him terribly. Sure enough, he shuddered, hands tightening on me. "Then I shall have to be sure to return to you."

He tensed, then set me away from him, holding me by the shoulders. "I'm coming with you."

"No." I said it very firmly. "This is mine to do, I must go alone." As Kaja would have. The certainty filled me. Danu's voice? I didn't know that, but I knew this was mine alone to accomplish.

"That's insane."

"Possibly. I've been trying to explain to you that I'm not all in my right mind." I laid a finger over the mouth he opened to argue with me. "I cannot risk having anyone with me, because if I lose myself and kill all around me, I would never forgive myself if I hurt someone I love. Like you."

"The words are not sounding so sweet to me now," he replied with some bitterness.

"If I'm to pay this debt and return to some semblance of a happy life, I won't be able to if that happens."

"I won't let you hurt me."

"I can't take that chance. If you won't promise to let me go alone, then I'll steal away and not say goodbye." I waited, watching his face, and knowing full well that I'd laid that threat tightly against his most sensitive wantings. *Ah, Hulda, how well you taught me.*

"I'll follow if you do," he replied, raising the stakes.

I shook my head, smiling. "You know I can move without leaving a trace. There will be no trail to follow, *and*," I interrupted him again before he could argue, "I swear to Danu that if you follow me, I will never come back here and will never be your wife."

He regarded me with some astonishment—and more than a little betrayal. It hurt my heart to see it, to know I caused it, but not as much as it would if I returned to my senses to find him dead at my feet, killed by my own blade. I held fast to that horrible image, using it to bolster my determination.

"I didn't imagine you could ever give me such an ultimatum," he said softly.

I stepped out of his hands and gave him a deep and formal curtsy, the gray gown and veil oddly like the klúts I'd worn when I'd last done that. "Her Highness Imperial Princess Jenna Konyngrr, at your service." I straightened. "I come from a family of ruthless people, on both sides. I wouldn't blame you if you decide you can't love that after all. In many ways, you don't truly know me."

He pressed his lips together, stricken. "I *want* to truly know you. If you go and don't return, how can that happen?"

I smiled, relief that he still wanted me like the sunshine after the rains. "If I don't do this, we maybe wouldn't have the time anyway. I've heard Desta talking, the other men—even you when you thought I wasn't listening—all of you think we cannot withstand the forces the Chimtoans can muster. We could lose all of Nyambura—the homes, our stores, the elephants, all the children. We'd have no time to know each other then, either."

Regarding me somberly, he pinched his nose between his fingers and thumb. "I had no idea you possessed such a ruthless view of the world."

"I am Dasnarian," I reminded him.

"And I love you," he said on a long sigh. "Which means I must accept this plan, however crazed. Is there nothing at all you will let me do to help you?"

"Yes, there is." I eased closer to him again, laying my palms flat on his chest, savoring the heat of his skin through the thin cloth, the crisp resilience of his chest hair. "In case I should live but be unable to return for some reason, I'd like you to plant your child in me."

~ 22 ~

He looked at me with such a combination of horror, arousal, despair, hope, and sheer bewilderment that I nearly laughed. I might have, if it wouldn't be so cruel. I might be like my mother in many ways, but not in that. Never in that.

"How?" he finally managed to ask, which was not the answer I'd expected.

"I thought you understood the mechanics," I teased, but he didn't smile back.

"I won't rape you," he said, flatly, and removing my hands from him, stepping out of my reach.

"It wouldn't be rape if I ask you to do it," I pointed out, a bit terse with annoyance that he'd make me fight him on this.

"So now, all of a sudden, you're certain you can enjoy bedding me? That you could take me inside your body and feel joyful?"

"Yes," I replied stubbornly. I could fake joy, pretend long enough to get through it. It would be worth it, to have his child, just in case.

He eased closer, a strange glint in his eye. "You'll just strip naked and open your legs for me. Lie back and let me mount you, pressing you down with my weight, thrusting my cock into you and—"

"Stop!" I had my hands over my ears, cringing as if he'd indeed beaten me. My stomach heaved, and if I'd eaten more than a few bites of fruit I might've puked right there.

Ochieng had his arms around me, holding me loosely but with warm affection, murmuring reassurances. "La, Ivariel. Shh. Don't weep. I'm sorry."

I caught my breath and moved my hands to my face, furiously wiping away the traitorous tears that had sprung up out of nowhere.

"I'm sorry, my love," he repeated. "I only meant to make a point. Which I think has been made. You're not ready for that. You can't even think about it."

"I don't have to think about it if you'll just do it," I insisted.

"Don't even suggest I would."

"It would be worth it." I leaned back to look at him. "To make a child, wouldn't it be worth it? You could put my face in a blanket in case I screamed, take me from behind and it would be over—"

"*No!*" He thrust me away from him as if burned. "Don't ever ask that of me again."

"Ochieng, I would—"

"Absolutely not." He glared at me, furiously offended. "I'd rather take a knife to myself than do that to you. Nothing is worth hurting you like that."

I put my hands on my hips. I'd gone from a husband who'd treated my body as a toy to break to one who wouldn't help me make a child for fear of upsetting me. "I thought you wanted children with me."

He gave me an incredulous look. "I do. *With* you. Someday, when they can be conceived in joy. What you're suggesting is me forcing you through a threshold you need to find a way across on your own."

"All right." I held up my hands in a calming gesture as he seemed anything but. "What about if you insert your seed in me another way."

He opened his mouth. Closed it again. Bent his head to study the floor a moment, then looked at me again. "*Insert another way?*" He still sounded dangerous, but I forged on.

"My late husband did that. With various… implements." And it had hurt. Sliced me and made me bleed. But I'd lived through it before without the reward of a child.

Ochieng's face had gone curiously blank, but that muscle in his jaw twitched. "Tell me."

I didn't think he really wanted to know. "It's not important if it's not something you want to try."

"Oh, it's important." He said it so quietly that I might've missed the fury beneath, if I hadn't begun to know his body so well.

"Why are you so angry at me?" I whispered.

He scrubbed his hands over his face, then came to me and took my hands, leading me to the pallet bed to sit, easing himself beside me. Still holding my hands—albeit tightly—but otherwise not touching me, he said, "I'm not angry at you. Not about that part, anyway. But it's difficult to hear what that monster did to you. I wish I could dismember him for you, and I … can't."

I swallowed, impossibly moved. "We won't speak of it then."

"Not speaking of it won't mean it isn't in your mind. Tell me about this. I want to know. At least let me share some part of this burden with you, even if you won't share anything else."

That seemed unfair, but I had brought it up. To me it hadn't seemed the worst of what my late husband had done to me. Still, my mouth went dry when I went to speak the words. Which meant Ochieng likely had a point about me holding still for the actual act. And I didn't think I could suffer having him tie me down, not even for this. The demon inside stirred in affirmation, and I knew she'd go for her knives.

"He would use carved implements, and put his seed inside them, or coat them with it, then thrust them inside me."

Ochieng nodded, face carefully neutral, so I continued. "They had spines on them, sharp things. I couldn't always see… but they hurt. He said… He said the blood helped with fertility. Like cats, you know, and—" I couldn't quite catch my breath. "And—"

Ochieng held my hands so tightly his grip nearly bruised, and his dark eyes burned like Danu's fire. "Is there more?" He'd steeled himself to ask that, I thought.

"Not about that part," I told him, glad not to have to explain further—and curiously lighter for having spoken that bit aloud. "Is it true, though—about the blood?"

He closed his eyes briefly, then shook his head. "No. It isn't. We are not cats."

"I kind of thought as much. None of the other women or my teachers had mentioned that part, but I had no one to ask."

"You didn't talk to your mother or your sisters about what was happening to you?"

I laughed a little, without humor. "My mother knew all the ways to cover the cuts and bruises so I could go back again the next night. My sisters… no, I didn't talk to them about it."

"Why not?" Ochieng had a tight leash on himself, but his voice grated.

"I didn't want them to be frightened." I lifted my shoulder in a shrug. "I was the eldest, the first to marry, and I didn't want them to know…" My voice broke, and I sobbed, a gut-wrenching, convulsive dry sobbing that tore out of me without my permission. "To know… how awful…"

Ochieng pulled me into his arms, holding me fiercely, no longer gentle or careful. "La, all right. Enough for now." His voice came out ragged and I didn't mind. That he felt for me helped me wrestle down my own jaggedness.

"I'm sorry," I breathed. "But thank you."

He laughed a little. "I don't know what you're thanking me for, but you have no reason to be sorry. It's hard, yes, to hear these things. Still I want to hear them, to share them."

"That's why I say thank you." I leaned into him. "And, you should know, because of... all that—I think I'm scarred."

"Oh, my love. I know. It's all right. I don't mind."

"I mean down there, in my woman parts. I bled a lot and my poor brother had to put stitches in me." I laughed, remembering. "The poor boy was only fourteen and had never seen a woman's intimates. I think *he* may be scarred for life."

"He is a good man," Ochieng said fervently. "I hope one day to meet him. And I don't care about any scarring, only that you suffered it."

"I think I could maybe still have a baby, though," I said hopefully. "I have my woman's courses. That's why I thought, if we could make a baby now, and I'm unable to return, then..." I trailed off because Ochieng had pulled back, that *look* on his face again.

"Yes, let's talk about that part. This 'in case you're unable to return.' What are you thinking there?"

I hesitated. He seemed more on edge than ever, despite the apparent calmness of his question. "I don't know where Danu will guide my feet," I offered tentatively. "I've been captured before. Gone away to lands I didn't even know the names of. It could happen again."

"Like a piece of storm wreckage, washed downriver," he suggested.

Tentatively, I nodded.

He exploded. Rocketed up and away from me. Pacing. "You are not passive wreckage, Ivariel!" he nearly shouted. I hoped no one could hear us, though I didn't know how they couldn't. "*You* determine the course of your life. Not a goddess. Not the forces of nature. *You.*"

I held my tongue, refraining from pointing out that my experience thus far in life indicated otherwise. He stormed on, not needing my reply anyway.

"And, thinking this, you want to bring a baby into such a life? Raise them without a home or plan. What role do I play in this scenario of yours, other than 'planting my seed' in you? Then you'd maybe be out there in the world somewhere, alone with our child, raising them without me. Don't you know me well enough to understand how that would slowly eat me alive?"

I stared at him, never having seen him so distraught. Eyes wild, hands waving, face contorted in such a rictus of emotions I couldn't put a name to them all. Such hidden depths to my sunny laughing storyteller. And he was right—about my failings and my short-sightedness.

"I apologize," I said quietly. "I didn't think this through."

He laughed, a bitter sound with a crazed edge. "No. No, you really didn't."
With a heavy sigh, I stood and went to my things, first rolling up the
knives again.

"What are you doing?" he asked, sounding exasperated but less wild.

I glanced at him, assessing, and he seemed calmer. "I'm packing up
my things."

"You plan to leave in the dead of night, without supplies, or saying
farewell to your family?" He pretended to be neutral, but the lethal edge
to his question arrested me.

"Actually, no," I replied. "Because you promised to let me go alone, I
hoped to gather supplies and say goodbye to everyone in the morning." *My
family.* "But I thought you'd want me to sleep elsewhere tonight. After all
of this," I gestured at the room, as if all of our angry and hurtful words lay
scattered on the floor where we'd flung them.

"Ivariel." He said my name on a long-suffering sigh. Then came to me,
drawing me to my feet. "Leave that. You asked me how people who love
each other fight. They don't do it by walking away. They say what they need
to, work out the path going forward, and then they make up to each other."

"Oh." I assimilated that. "I think we've said what we need to. And worked
out the path going forward, more or less."

"More or less," he agreed with a slight smile. "As best we can, anyway."

"What's involved in making up to each other?" I purred the question,
because I suspected I knew.

His smile widened. "Would you come to bed with me, sleep by my side?"

"Yes." I leaned in and kissed him, mostly a test of his feelings toward me,
gratified when he returned the kiss with fervor. With the heat and flavor
I'd come to think of as the taste and feel of love. "And I will pleasure you,
to make it up to you."

He cupped my face in his hands, expression going serious. "I'd like to
try to pleasure you."

I stilled, despite my earlier bravado, a chill of concern going through
me. "I don't know..."

"We can take it slowly, but I'd like to try." He smiled now, sadness in it. "If
only to give you something to take with you. Incentive to come back to me."

"I already have ten thousand reasons to come back to you."

"Then let me give you a few more."

Taking me by the hand, he led me to his bed.

~ 23 ~

He pulled off his gray shirt and pants, standing there entirely naked, since he'd long-since doffed the head covering. Moving closer, I reached behind his neck to untie the lace holding his hair in the queue. He held still for me, eyes full of deep emotion as I combed the hair free with my fingers, then lightly kissed him.

"May I undress you, my Ivariel?" he asked, the question sounding almost like a formal request.

I shifted my weight from foot to foot, then stilled myself, as the movement reminded me of Efe's anxious dancing. "I have scars," I reminded him.

"I don't mind the scars," he reminded me, in turn.

"All right," I said, steeling myself.

"Relax," he murmured. "Only pleasure. Only love." He kissed me, with that tenderness that clouded my mind as sweetly as the opos smoke had done, but instead of dragging me into numbness, his caresses brought me to singing awareness. His clever fingers drifted over my bare arms, as if savoring the feel of my skin. Raising them to my hair, he unpinned the mourning veil I'd forgotten I wore, letting it drift to the floor. I drifted, too, letting my head fall back so his mouth could cruise along my throat, awakening delicious feelings in me, such as I'd never experienced.

I sighed, partly in relief, largely in delight. He murmured some reply, happy to have pleased me. His hands ran over my body in long, slow strokes that dissolved the last of my tension. *Precious to me.* That's how he made me feel. I didn't even flinch—indeed, barely noticed—when he found the ties at my shoulders and undid them. The gray gauzy gown whispered to my feet, and I stood there naked in a pool of it.

His hands continued to glide over me in the same way as before, but the exquisite feel of his skin against mine created a new chorus of song in my body. To my surprise, my sex warmed and grew wet for him. Amazing that such simple touching could do such a thing. He followed his hands with his mouth, pressing kisses to my shoulder, the hollow of my breastbone, the inside of my wrist and elbow. I'd done this for him and yet hadn't understood how it unraveled one from the deepest core outward.

He paused, hands sliding up and down my back as he studied my face. "All good?"

"All wonderful," I breathed.

Smiling, radiant with it, sharing that relief with me, he slid his hands around my waist, nearly able to span it with his long fingers. Then slowly brought them up, watching my face all the while, until he cupped my breasts. I took in a breath at the startling sensation, and he drew his brows together. "No?"

"Yes." I really didn't want him to stop. "I had no idea it could feel so... good. I wish I knew more words."

He chuckled, mouth going a little wicked, eyes sparkling. "Words only say so much."

"This from you?" I gasped as he brushed his thumbs over my taut nipples, grabbing ahold of his strong shoulders, as I felt suddenly dizzy. "Ochieng!"

He laughed again, caressing my breasts, then gently rolling my nipples between thumb and forefinger. "You like this?"

I could only moan in response, the keen pleasure obliterating my mind.

"I have no special tutoring," he teased, speaking against my skin as his mouth flowed down my throat, tongue hot on my breasts. "I cannot brag of how you can tell the world you've been pleasured by Ochieng D'tiembo." And then he took my nipple in his mouth, sucking on it, and I cried out, my knees collapsing. He caught my weight easily, and grinned at me. "But I think I'm doing well enough."

"Yes," I managed to say. "That was more than wonderful."

"Oh, I'm not done yet. Not after how you tormented me this morning."

Had it only been that morning? The day had lasted forever. So many changes. I let him guide me to the bed, lying down as he urged me, facing him as he laid himself beside me.

"Is this good?" he asked running a hand down my flank, over the round of my hip and along my thigh, his eyes following the caress before rising to look into mine, assessing.

"So far, yes."

"Good," he murmured, easing me onto my back and rising onto his elbow. He ran his free hand from my throat to my breasts, smoothing and teasing them, then down my belly, his expression intent as he did. Then he looked into my face. "Still good?"

I nodded, and he stilled. "Something wrong?"

"No. Yes." I pressed my lips together, afraid he'd stop. "It's just… I used to be beautiful."

"Oh, my Ivariel." Deliberately he let his gaze wander over my body. "You are so breathtakingly beautiful that you shatter me. I cannot get enough of seeing, touching and tasting you." He followed with his mouth, demonstrating with reverent sensuality, and I let the susurrus of sensation take me under.

On some dim level, I recognized he'd turned around some of my same tricks on me, leveraging the long, slow and deliberate teasing to make me lose all reserve. Fair enough, I figured, as I registered in the back of my mind those things I'd like to try on him.

By the time he made his way to the nest of ivory curls at my mons, I was panting and ready to give him anything he asked to end the delightful torment, not resisting in the slightest when he parted my knees, kissing his way with painstaking thoroughness up the tender insides of my thighs.

I stopped him though, when he parted my folds, skimming his fingers through the moisture there. He lifted his head when I put my hands on his shoulders. His eyes shone with dark arousal and sweet concern. "All right?" he asked, his voice hoarse with the same desire that thrummed through me.

"Yes." In truth, I'd never imagined I could feel this way, that a woman could experience this kind of transporting pleasure. "But… tell me the truth. Is it bad? I haven't been able to see myself there, so … I want to know."

He turned his head, kissing my thigh, pressing the kiss there. "You are perfect, my love, in every way." Then he turned his gaze to my open sex, stroking the hair and the tender petals of it with a smile on his generous mouth, one that widened as I undulated with the caress, a whimper escaping me. "And you are beautiful here, too. A delicate pink, like an exotic flower. A few scars, fine white lines, but nothing to worry about. You look healthy and lovely here as everywhere."

I sighed with relief, letting my head drop back. "Thank you."

"Hold that thought," he said, voice full of smug male pride, "as you'll be wanting to truly sing my praises in a few more moments."

Did he think to bring me to the same kind of completion that men experienced? Because I didn't think it worked the same way. "Ochieng, you don't have—" I lost my words in a most unladylike *guh* of mind-shattering sensation as his mouth closed on my sex.

He might've chuckled, but he continued, kissing and licking me there, finding that pearl of intense pleasure and sucking on it with all the finesse of the most finely trained rekjabrel. I thrashed, bucking my hips, and he followed along, chasing me and not trying to pin me in place. I dug my nails into his shoulders, pleading wordlessly, feeling the unbearable tension rise, and rise, and rise...

Until I came apart. The world spun as if I danced at manic speeds, the light and sound and scent and sensation spiraling in a mix brighter than the stars, more profound than the blackest depths of the ocean. Fiery sparks rained through my mind, my voice keening the intensity of the pleasure he brought to me.

* * * *

He eased me down, showering my skin with kisses as he made his way up my body, murmuring words of love and admiration. I felt languid, suffused with happiness, my mind drifting with perfect ease. It was as if all those girlish dreams of the handsome prince and some vaguely glorious happy ever after had condensed themselves into this single moment.

With great care, I rolled all that feeling into a shining sphere, like a pearl beyond price, and tucked it into my memory box.

Then I curled into Ochieng, savoring the feel of his body against mine. His cock lay hard and hot against my belly and I reached for it, to relieve his need, but he stopped me with a gentle hand. Then he kissed me on my forehead, lips lingering there as if bestowing a blessing.

"Enough for tonight," he murmured.

"Are you sure?" I tipped my head back a little, seeing the same effervescent pleasure in his eyes as thrummed through my body. "We could try for a little more." It occurred to me that he hadn't penetrated me in any way, not with fingers or tongue, even.

"We're not going there again." He still looked happy and satiated, but the tone of finality in his voice gave me warning. "Besides," he added with a smile, "I need to give you plenty of reasons to come back to me."

I knew he was teasing me, but I cupped his face in my hands. "There are all the reasons in the world," I said. "I'll be back, even if it takes me twenty years."

He laid a finger over my lips. "Don't speak of such an extremity. In fact, if you're not back in twenty days, I'm coming after you." He shook his head when I opened my mouth to protest, then pressed a kiss to the palm of my hand. "If you haven't returned by then, your ultimatum will no longer hold power over me. I will come after you."

I'd have to make sure he didn't have to.

~ 24 ~

Just before dawn, I crept out while Ochieng still slept. I dressed in my leathers, the feel of the tighter clothing both familiar and strange. Unrolling the leather case holding my knives, I took a breath, searching myself. No angry serpent flared her hood, but the quiet resolve I associated with the presence of Danu filled my mind.

All right then. My hands remembered, strapping the knives into their places, then the sword belt. I buckled on my vambraces, not because I wished to hide my scars still, but because they reminded me of who Kaja had helped me grow to be. The rest of that would be up to me.

I stood a moment, admiring Ochieng's masculine beauty as he slept, so deeply and peacefully that I wanted nothing more than to undress and curl up next to him again. Only the knowledge that such peace would be doomed to a brief existence stopped me. My curse would chase me to this place and rip everything away from me again. I'd run as far and as fast as I could, but it always came after me. It was time for me to turn around and face what pursued me.

Not to surrender this time, but to defeat it.

Carrying my boots, I stealthily slid back the cover to the stairs just enough to slip through, pushing it back into place again. I made my way through the quiet house, nodding good morning to the other early risers. Their sharp eyes took note of my reversion, but no one said anything. Until Zalaika.

She was coming up the stairs from the storehouse, carrying a huge basket of fruit. I couldn't have dodged her if I tried. The brief wish that I could've gone down the cliff stairs flitted through my mind, quickly followed by a tinge of regret that I might never use them again. They'd be fixed, but I might not be here.

"Good morning, Zalaika," I said, a bit more formally than I meant to.

"Priestess Ivariel." She inclined her head to me, and I realized she acknowledged my return to my office and duty to Danu—and seemed totally unsurprised. "You'll be checking on Capa, then?" she asked.

"Yes." I hadn't been able to see the elephant on the beach from Ochieng's room.

"Good." She nodded and moved past me.

"Zalaika," I said, then hesitated. I'd never learned how to express regret over loss. In Dasnaria any such words would likely be taken as a taunt. "I am so very sorry that Femi died."

She gave me a long look. Smudges of the crimson paint remained in the fine lines at the corners of her eyes and mouth, as if she'd washed it off half-heartedly. "You'll make sure they don't take any more of my children."

"I will," I promised, even though I had no idea how I'd do that.

"Good," she said, exactly as she had before, as if seeking out and killing the Chimtoans would be just another errand like checking on an injured elephant. Perhaps it was. She paused, then reached out to cup my cheek. "We shall hold the festival for your return, and then you shall marry my son and formalize this marriage you've already consummated, yes?"

I blushed and she broke into a broad grin, patting my cheek. "Life goes on, Priestess. Look—the sun rises yet again, as it does every day. Go destroy your monsters and come home to us."

* * * *

The sky lightened into bright pinks as I set foot on the beach at last, mist swirling over the river. Many of the elephants had already waded into the water, though Violet still stood over Capa. To my surprise, Efe was with them, too. She gamboled over when she spotted me, swinging her trunk merrily, wrapping me in a hug with it, delighted when I plucked a melon from the basket of food I'd brought for Capa and gave it to her.

Happily munching, she accompanied me back to Capa, who lay unmoving. At first I held my breath in dread, not able to see her breath in the misty dimness. If she'd died in the night, what would that omen mean for my journey—warning that I shouldn't go, or emphasizing that I should?

As I approached, singing a bit of the elephant song, she opened her eye and let out a long whuff of air. "La, Capa," I crooned. "Still abed with the sun rising? So lazy!"

She lifted her trunk, waving it at me weakly. "I know, honey. I've been there and it's terrible." I waved a piece of fruit over the tip of her trunk, trying to tempt her. "You must be hungry."

But she wouldn't take it, so I laced up the basket to keep the other curious elephants out of it, and set it aside.

I found a clear space on the beach, and commenced my prayers to Glorianna, as Kaja had taught me to do. And I poured my self into them, hoping to communicate my supplication for Her blessing, the fervency of my hope. When I'd first fled Dasnaria, I'd found it so difficult to hope for anything. Hiding in my darkened cabin, I'd practiced with tiny, unimportant hopes, thinking of them as baby steps to carry me on to bigger ones. Thinking I might someday discover what I hoped for myself.

Now hope had descended upon me with full-blown and blistering immediacy. I knew what I wanted: to sleep in Ochieng's arms every night, to share pleasure with him and bear our children, to become a D'tiembo in truth and spend my life caring for the elephants, to stand as guardian for this peaceful verdant valley, and to make myself into someone powerful enough to go back and liberate my sisters someday. So many hopes and yet all the same hope.

And the great burning desire to make that true rose in me like the fiery sun topping the hills beyond the river. Seamlessly I moved into the ducerse, drawing my sword at the moment I would've opened my palms to the pearls I'd once balanced there, and dancing my fealty to Danu.

Clear mind. Clear heart. And my sword sworn to Danu's justice, whatever it may be. *And none shall harm me because Danu travels in my heart, in my mind, and in my blade.*

I finished with Danu's salute, the goddess's blessing coursing white-hot through me with the morning light, making me wonder how I'd ever doubted Her hand on me. Lowering myself from pointed toe, I turned to find Ochieng waiting quietly, an inscrutable expression on his face.

"When I woke and found you gone, I thought you might've stolen away in the night again," he said.

"I promised I wouldn't."

"I know." He didn't comment on the fact that he'd thought I'd promised before. We understood each other better now. I hoped. He stood, uncoiling himself from his seated position, then coming to kiss me. "You moved well."

"I feel good."

"Back to the terrifyingly intimidating Warrior Priestess Ivariel, ever cool and silent, scourge of the oasis ruffians—and all others who threaten her and those she loves."

I didn't laugh, as he no doubt expected by bringing up what he'd said to me when I fell off Violet on my ass, amusing him greatly. Instead, I considered him, and how he described me. "I never felt like that inside."

"It must be who you are, because that's what shines through. It's who you are to the core of your being."

"I haven't been at all sure if there's anything at the core of my being beyond this... hurt and hatred." That's how it had felt, under the cloying layers of rotting memories, the familiar serpent lurking, waiting to strike.

He ran a hand over my hair, giving me a serious smile. "I think I've been as close to you as one person can be to another and I can promise that there's more to you than that."

"How can you know?"

"Because you are who you were before your mother hurt you, before your late husband brutalized you. Think back to that girl. What was she like?"

Could it be that yet another self lay beneath all that muck, somehow buried deeper still? I remembered that day in the seraglio, playing games with my brother Kral, before he grew up to be my enemy. We'd looked at the tapestry showing elephants in a parade—in what I now recognized as battle regalia, in my mind's eye—and all I'd wanted was to know about them. As if reading my thoughts, Efe snaked her trunk through my arm tugging at me, and I hugged her back.

She kept tugging though, so I turned to look at her. "Silly girl, what?" Then saw past her. "Ochieng," I breathed.

He sucked in a breath, then let it out in a whoop. And we ran, all three of us, to Capa, who was struggling to her feet.

We helped as best we could, answering her questing trunk, reassuring her. Violet moved against Capa's far flank, helping her find her balance. Capa wound her trunk around my head, then dusted it down over my hands, making an annoyed huff when she found them empty. Laughing, I told her to wait a moment while I fetched and unlaced the basket.

Grinning at me with full delight, Ochieng fed Capa from the basket— and slipping something to the hopefully hovering Efe now and again. We lingered there a while, savoring at least this one happy outcome, until all the fruit was gone and Capa fell into a doze. The sun had risen high, and Ochieng caught me glancing at it.

"It's time for you to be going," he said, part question, part realization.

"Yes." I patted Capa's flank, feeling that this had to be a good omen. "I have to do this."

He closed his eyes briefly, then opened them, giving me a long look. "I know you do."

* * * *

They all gathered to say goodbye, all the D'tiembos and others, and the elephants, including Efe and Bimyr. Violet had stayed with Capa down on the beach, which was right and good. Besides the traveling bags I'd arrived with, several big panniers of supplies sat at the ready. I frowned at them, turning to ask what I was supposed to do with those, when a small body hurtled herself at me.

"La, Ayela!" I laughed, her arms tight around my waist with all the mighty fury of a kitten. "You about knocked the breath out of me."

She tilted her chin up, dark eyes fierce. "I'm going with you. I just need my knife back."

"The knife you 'borrowed' without asking?" I raised my brows at her, glad to see her look at least a little chagrined. I hadn't wanted to chastise her before now, but it needed to be said. Kaja would expect that, at the very least.

"I'm sorry, Priestess Ivariel," Ayela said solemnly. "But only that I took it without permission, not that I had it because then you killed the bad men with it. Maybe Danu guided my hand in this."

"Maybe so," I agreed with equal gravity, much as I wanted to smile at her clever borrowing of my words. Maybe Danu had reached Ayela through me. That was part of my vow to Her. And who was I to question the hand of the goddess? "And thus"—I drew that knife from my belt and presented it to her, as I wished I'd been able to do when I left before, but couldn't because I'd snuck away—"here is your knife, as all students should receive their first from their teacher. Use it well."

She took it with reverence. "I can go with you?"

"No, this is something I have to do alone, but you may keep it and stand guard over your family in my place. Will you do that for me?"

Eyes huge in her young face, she nodded. Just a little younger than I'd been when my mother taught me the only way I'd escape her power was to marry and become empress in my own right. But I'd learned otherwise. I'd escaped her. Finally and fully. Now it only remained for me to find my own power. However I'd manage that.

"I cannot possibly take all of this stuff," I said to the D'tiembo family, pointing to the big panniers that only an elephant could carry, still amused and touched by their gesture.

"You can if you ride Bimyr," Palesa told me. "We've all agreed."

"These are supplies, for the needy and deserving of Chimto," Thanda added. "In case you're able to give them. If you find a way to defeat the warriors"—her gaze slid to Desta, who returned it impassively—"then we can send more."

It surprised me that they still wanted to help the people who'd murdered our people, attacking us without cause. Palesa read it in me and nodded. "What matters is our intention, yes? Who we wish to be in the world. Not what they try to force us to be out of their own pain and misery."

"We'd rather send you on Violet," Zalaika put in, "but Capa needs her."

"Oh yes, Capa definitely needs Violet," I replied, "but you cannot send Bimyr with me. You need her here to mount a defense of Nyambura, just in case."

"Ivariel," Ochieng inserted in a firm voice. "You cannot think to walk all that way. Take one of the elephants."

"I walked all the way here from Bandari," I pointed out to him, raising my eyebrow.

"Not alone," he returned in the same tone. "You need a friend with you."

"It's not good to go alone," Desta agreed, giving me a significant look, so I shouldn't have been surprised that he agreed. Or that all of the D'tiembos considered having an elephant companion as taking a friend along. Such a generous gift and yet... how could I?

"But you need all the fighting elephants to—" I broke off when Efe stuck her trunk through my arm, tugging at me. Danu's sun shone down from the noon sky, making Efe shine like silver in the bright light. No mud on her at all, I realized. And I knew that Efe also had her own scars, her own wounds to reclaim. Just how smart were elephants? As wise, perhaps, as that seven-year-old girl who lay at the core of me. The girl who'd looked at an image of an elephant in wonder—and maybe somehow foresaw this day would come. "What if I take Efe?"

Several people laughed, but Ochieng didn't. Palesa, Thanda, and Zalaika exchanged glances. And Efe... she smiled at me, still tugging at my arm.

"Will she let you ride her?" Ochieng asked, watching us steadily. Something about the question reminded me of the day he taught me to ride Violet. *Clear heart. Clear mind. Eyes where you want to be.* That was a mashing-up of his advice and Kaja's, and yet it felt right, like something I'd made my own.

That thought resonated through me like a gong in the quiet of Danu's temple. Something there. I needed to take all of it, all of the pieces of me, and make them one thing all my own.

"Yes," I told him. "Yes, she will." I signaled Efe to kneel, and she did, with as much perfect grace as if she'd practiced it a thousand times. She'd known what she was supposed to do; she just hadn't had it in her to bear it before this. Or maybe—like me—not a good enough reason to push past the fear.

I climbed up, mindful of my boot heels, and sang her a standing song, then a walking tune. We paraded in a circle, Efe with me as if of one mind. Thank Danu. Or perhaps gratitude went to Moranu, as animals belonged to Her. I would have to get better at meditating, as I tended to leave the goddess of shadows out of my prayers. Just as I'd wanted to divorce myself of my own darkness.

This new resonance made me think perhaps the path forward lay in embracing that dark serpent rather than exorcising it.

Asking Efe to kneel again, I slid off, then helped the others load the panniers onto her. She allowed the straps and waited patiently as if she'd done this all her life. The others commented on her change, but I paid little attention to their discussion. The time to say goodbye to Ochieng had come, and I almost couldn't bear it.

"You're not surprised," I said to him, as a stalling tactic.

He lifted his shoulder and let it fall, a very Dasnarian shrug, then grinned at me, all him. "I had a feeling. And I have something for you." Stepping into an alcove, he returned with something large and dark in his hands. A hat, woven of dark-colored grasses, a deep purple blue that looked black until the sun shone on it. With a sense of ceremony, he set the hat on my head, settling it for me and brushing the brim with his fingers, as if to make it exactly right.

"Beautiful," he said.

I blinked back tears. These felt like good tears, though, not the helpless outpouring of grief that had so seized me all these months. "When did you get this?"

"I had someone in town make it for you, since you lost the other. I know it's not jewels, but—"

"But I've had jewels and this is better." I kissed him. "Thank you. I love you."

"Come back to me," he murmured fervently, holding on a moment longer.

"I will," I told him. "I promise."

~ 25 ~

At first, Efe and I traveled through the busy part of the town, people waving to us as they continued their work in making repairs from the rains—and recovering from the attack. But quickly we left the sprawling houses on stilts for the already sprouting fields. I followed the map Ochieng had given me, proud that I could read it, taking the river road, heading downstream, leaving the people and town behind.

It felt odd to be alone again. I'd become accustomed to having someone in the family if not within eyesight, then at least within shouting distance. Half a dozen times words sprang to my lips to point out some sight to Ochieng, or ask him a question, and I discovered through his absence how very much I'd come enjoy his companionship.

Not something I'd ever expected to have, not even when I believed I'd rule beside my someday husband. Also something my mother had never known to teach me, because she'd never had it. Strange to contemplate my mother, as Efe and I rode along the river road at a brisk pace. She'd married young—younger than I had—and would be about Thanda's age. And yet my mother possessed the matriarchal gravity of Zalaika, and more so. Perhaps being empress had made her that way. More likely the same sort of miseries visited on me had made her hard and cruel in turn.

I could understand that now, because I could see that path before me. If I allowed the monster inside me to slay everything else that I was, I'd become as ruthless. Hurt before you are hurt. Power is everything. Power is all that protects you.

The lessons whispered through my mind as if my mother spoke them still. For the first time I recognized that—as much as she'd injured me, and used me for her own ends—in many ways she'd also thought she was giving me the tools I needed to survive what my life would be. She hadn't been able to imagine my life being anything but the same as hers. In her way, she'd equipped me for that, much as Kaja had put a blade in my hand.

Now it would be up to me to find the path to being someone strong, but not cruel. That dark serpent of hatred that made it so easy to kill gave me strength and power. Moranu brought that gift of darkness, of animal ruthlessness. Glorianna mitigated that, Her love leavening the darkness, Her light rising from it and keeping it from consuming everything. And Danu…She brought the clear-eyed wisdom to balance the others, to create justice where there had been none.

* * * *

I slept that night under the stars, curled under Efe's chin, very glad of her company. Though I'd slept outdoors like this on the journey from Bandari, being without the caravan under the night sky became an entirely different effort. To diffuse my creeping fear, I meditated, offering gratitude to Moranu. The goddess of the night has no formal prayers, because She is also anarchy. Where Danu draws a clear line, Moranu is without boundaries. Of the three sisters, I understood Moranu the least, but I offered Her my attention—and my apologies for cursing Her dark face—hoping She would understand that I'd had to grow to understand that aspect.

We traveled all the next day, and I walked as much as I rode. Efe and I moved at about the same speed—a brisk walk for me, a comfortable pace for her—but I found walking helped me vent the building anxiety. I had sort of a plan, but no idea what I'd find when I reached Chimto. I wondered if Kaja had felt this way on her travels, and then thought that she must have. She'd always been exhorting me to both be alert and to give myself over to Danu's guiding hand.

It took a great leap of faith, but I supposed that had been her point all along. Trust in myself; trust in the goddess. Clear mind. Clear heart. Eyes on where you want to go.

* * * *

The following morning we traveled into the rising sun. The river had turned due east, where Ochieng had told me his ancestor came from. By late morning, I began to see other elephants as we drew closer to Chimto. These elephants wore great manacles, however, metal cuffs that showed on their

150

Jeffe Kennedy

ankles even from a distance, and the clanking of the chains that connected them echoed across the fields.

At first I worried that Efe would see the manacles and panic, remembering the ones that had bound her and left her scarred. The scars on my own wrists seemed to itch under the vambraces in sympathy, though that had to be my imagination. Elephant minds must work differently than human ones do, however, because she only waved her trunk with interest at the sight of her kind, but continued along as I directed her.

As long as I kept calm possession of my self, Efe would do likewise. A challenge for me, especially as we began to pass people who gave me curious looks.

One advantage to me making this foray alone: I didn't look Nyamburan, or even Chiyajuan. Efe bore no identifying marks, and I presented myself as a Priestess of Danu. These people might not have heard of Danu, but they recognized me as foreign. *The terrifyingly intimidating Warrior Priestess Ivariel, ever cool and silent.* Ochieng's words whispered in my mind, and I tried to project that image of how he'd seen me.

The people I passed were mainly farmers, tradespeople, and other working folk like that. I'd expected ranks of warriors as I would have seen in Dasnaria. But no—wherever their armies were, they did not walk along the river road.

Instead I saw as many women as men, along with the elders and children, all out laboring in the fields or driving the *negombe* to pull carts up and down the road where it ran above water, though deeply rutted in mud more often than not. They, too, sang as they worked—or to move the *negombe* along—but their songs had a weary cast, and the fields often stood hip-deep in flood water still. The elephant chains worked to remove enormous piles of wreckage, on land and in the river, and I could see where detritus washed downstream had choked the current, forcing the river to find other ways around.

Even houses on stilts as in Nyambura had flooded, some standing like abandoned islands in dank-looking water. Possessions had been piled on the roofs, equally bedraggled, and in places groups of people huddled atop the roof beams, watching our passage with bleak expressions.

At one point, we passed a group of several dozen people struggling to push an entire house from what looked like a lake and onto higher ground. Efe watched with great interest, too, and I considered stopping to offer her might. Just then, however, the house moved—and I could see they'd put logs beneath it to make it roll—and they shouted in triumph, settling the house into its new location.

I waved, calling congratulations, and they shouted back their delight. It helped my heart to see some good amid the rest of the devastation. Some places looked to me as if they'd be better given over to the river entirely. I rode Efe right into the center of town. Chimto could even be called a city, rather than a town—nearly as large as Sjór, though nothing like Ehas—and was much more built up than sleepy Nyambura. Most of the structures sat on a wide, flat bluff well above the river, and so those buildings all appeared to be more or less intact. Also built primarily of wood, the center of Chimto looked more like a city of the Twelve Kingdoms or Dasnaria, and I found myself missing the breezier, open construction of houses upriver and toward Bandari.

With wide open, stone-cobbled streets, the city easily accommodated Efe's bulk, though I saw only a few other elephants, all manacled and chained. And here were the warriors, garbed like the ones who'd attacked us. They marched in the streets, and a large group gathered in what looked like the main square of town. They occasionally looked askance at me, but otherwise paid little attention. A lone woman on a scarred and relatively scrawny elephant surely posed no danger to them.

Still, I avoided them as best as I could, following the streets to the more attractive buildings, looking for the fancier neighborhoods, like Ehas had. In places where greed reigned, wealth meant power, and I meant to find the wealthiest man—or woman—in Chimto. That would bring in another face of myself, the one who'd learned the ways of power at her mother's side.

The house I found exceeded even my imaginings. Though it would still pale in comparison to the Imperial Palace in Dasnaria. This mansion stood upon the highest rise, enjoying a spectacular vista in all directions, with a tended garden arrayed around it like an empress's formal klút. A wall of stone surrounded the grounds, and guards stood at wrought-metal gates that looked like they could be locked.

I rode up, noting how they put hands on their swords, nodded regally and had Efe kneel so I could dismount. I could've simply slid down her flank, but I thought it important to demonstrate some formality and my control of her.

"That elephant should be chained," one of the guards snarled at me in the Chiyajuan trade tongue.

I smiled back, putting a hand under Efe's jaw to keep her still. "I'll stand surety for her behavior," I replied in the same language, a bit rustily, as I'd grown accustomed to the dialect they used in Nyambura.

"*You?*" the other guard sneered.

"One who cannot control their elephant is false with themselves," I replied easily, repeating something I'd heard often in Nyambura. They shifted uncomfortably, so I pursued my advantage. "I seek an audience with your master."

"And who is calling?" asked the first guard, not a challenge so much. I'd pulled on my best imperious attitude and if I'd learned little else at my mother's knee, I did know how to intimidate those who serve the powerful.

"Ivariel, Priestess of Danu. I come on a mission from the goddess."

The guards exchanged uncertain glances.

"Which involves gracing your master with wealth," I added nonchalantly. Prepared for this, I opened my hand to show a sparkle of small diamonds, ones I'd pried from the settings of my elaborate wedding bracelets. As quickly as I revealed them, I hid them away again, smiling serenely. "Your master *will* want to see me."

"Yes, Priestess," the one guard agreed, bobbing a bow. "If you'll come with me…"

The other guard protested in their dialect and the first, somewhat harshly, told him to keep his place. They opened the gates and I stayed on foot, my hand on Efe's jaw, walking beside the guard who escorted me.

We drew up to the house, which had inlaid steps leading up to a wide portico. The guard paused uncertainly. "We don't have a place for the elephant…"

"Could I wait outside—that arbor, perhaps?—I'm happy to receive your master there." It wasn't easy to find eloquently polite and yet firm command phrases in the Chiyajuan tongue, but I came pretty close.

The guard hesitated. I produced a small diamond. "For your trouble."

He smiled in delighted gratitude. "That arbor will be fine, Lady Priestess. I'll hurry to fetch Master Tamrat for you."

I thanked him, rather elaborately, then Efe and I strolled to the arbor. Everything in this garden dripped with flowers, plenty that I'd never seen before. If the poorer Chimtoans suffered deprivation, it didn't show here. Efe dusted the bright panicles of flowers with longing, huffing when I told her she'd better not. Instead I coaxed her to lie down in the shade, promising her a dip in the river later, and I stretched myself out next to her, deliberately relaxed, my hat mostly tipped over my eyes, as if I drowsed.

Mostly, because I could see just fine as the apparent master of this grand house emerged with the guard—and escorted by several more—frowning in my direction. He wore expensive silks that might have been imported from Dasnarian ships, and he glittered with jewels, though none so fine as mine, I suspected. Dismissing the gate guard, he strode in my direction, pausing a safe distance away.

"Wake up!" he demanded. "What is the meaning of this incursion?"

~ 26 ~

Keeping my movements languid, I gracefully tipped up my hat, taking my time to take his measure—and being sure he felt the weight of my imperial scrutiny. So many times my mother had used this ploy, fussing with her tea, appearing torn between napping and wasting her precious time on whatever person she'd summoned to her presence.

Master Tamrat tried to appear dignified, but fidgeted under my intense stare, put entirely off balance by my attitude and demeanor. The poor man had no idea the personage he dealt with. With a sigh, as if I'd decided I could be bothered at least to stand, I rose to my feet, employing all the strength and grace I possessed, rising as if from the deep bend of the ducerse, fluid, ethereal, lethal.

I let him see it all, using my height and imposing presence to best advantage. Cool and intimidating. "Master Tamrat?" I inquired as if I'd been expecting someone far more impressive.

"Yes," he bit out, clearly annoyed to be treated as my underling. Excellent.

"I am Ivariel, Warrior Priestess of Danu."

"I don't know this god of yours."

I smiled, ever so slightly, amused by his pathetic ignorance. "The goddess knows you. And She has empowered me to make you an offer, if you are indeed the most powerful man in Chimto?" I made it a question, implying he seemed lacking to my eye.

He puffed up. "I am. Your goddess has seen truly."

"Danu is the goddess of clear-sight," I acknowledged. "If you are indeed the man I seek, then I have a gift for you. I am in possession of a powerful artifact, one that has belonged to generations of kings and even an empress." I figured that little shading of the truth would harm none.

"Danu wishes you to have it, and it will bring you even greater fortune in the days ahead."

His fingers practically twitched with avarice, eyes gleaming with it—but he was no fool. I had to give the man that. "And what is the price for such a valuable 'gift'?"

I inclined my head, allowing a bit of allure to touch my smile. "I can see why you have risen to such a high position of wealth and power. You are wise as well as clever."

He preened a little at that, and I kept my shield of imperious indifference, pleased with myself that I was able to ignore the lust in his eyes as his gaze traveled over my body. "Perhaps you should come inside," he suggested. "Take refreshment with me. Your elephant will be safe here and we can... discuss the parameters of this enticing offer."

I managed not to laugh. He only wished. "The Priestesses of Danu are not for ordinary men," I told him, making it clear I'd manufactured the regret to buffer his ego. "And Her emissaries do not enter the abodes of non-believers, nor do they eat or drink of their households." After all, poison could be employed in any household. That center of me—Danu or my core self—agreed with the principle. "Also, there is nothing to discuss. Either you accept the gift and agree to what Danu requires in return. Or I shall leave." I lifted my shoulder and let it fall. "It matters not to me, as I've served the will of my goddess regardless."

Master Tamrat studied me, greed warring with caution. "Let me see this artifact."

Acting as if it mattered little to me, I withdrew the diamond ring from my pocket, holding it so the sunlight caught the glittering facets, making sure its obscene size was clear in relation to my hand. I'd cleaned and shined it up the night before, feeling much as I did polishing my sword. Both weapons to be employed, but one infinitely more useful.

Master Tamrat was too practiced to show his astonishment, but his men gasped and muttered. He threw them a silencing glance, then held out his hand. "May I examine it?"

I'd anticipated this and knew it would have to be handled delicately. Slipping it onto my finger—not my marriage finger, as I was too superstitious for that—I drew near and offered my hand. With a wry look for my caution, he took my hand, turning it to examine the jewel with an obviously expert eye.

"How came you by such an extraordinary piece?" He asked idly, but I recognized the stealthy attack for what it was.

I withdrew my hand. "Danu works in mysterious ways," I informed him, coldly enough to make it clear I'd tolerate no further questions.

"I see." His mind worked behind his pleasant smile, weighing his options. "And what bargain do you propose, Priestess?"

Ah-ah. I wanted to waggle my finger at him, but settled for bored authority. "The terms are immutable. Take them or don't. This jewel will bring you the fortune you seek and the succor of all the people of Chimto. In return, you will desist from attacking your neighbors. *All* of your neighboring clans."

His initial surprise—swiftly covered—changed to canny calculation. "What interest does a foreign goddess take in the backward clans of my country?"

"Do you pretend to know the mind of a goddess?" I asked with lofty scorn. "Suffice to say that elephants are sacred to Danu, and the people outside Chimto honor Her in their work with Her creatures."

"We value elephants also," he argued. "Surely you saw them on your journey from the countryside."

"You enslave them," I returned baldly, letting my contempt show. "Danu doesn't require that you free Her sacred creatures." I'd argued this point with myself, longing to make it one of the terms, but unwilling to push my luck beyond my primary mission. "However, you seem like a man who considers the future. Danu rewards those who treat elephants as their kin, not their slaves."

He studied me. "I am not the governor of Chimto. I do not order the warriors. Why approach me?"

I smiled, allowing him into my confidence. "Oh, come now, Master Tamrat. Surely I see before me not only a wealthy man, but a powerful one. You, I, and Danu know that you are the one to pull the strings of those who govern. You are humble to pretend otherwise, but I came to you first for a reason."

He laughed a little, acknowledging the truth of my words. "And if I refuse?"

With a sigh, I admired the diamond on my finger, then slipped it off and tucked it back into a pocket of my leathers. "Then I shall look for your competitor. Surely there are those who envy you and long to surpass you."

His face hardened despite himself, knowing I manipulated him and yet unable to extricate himself from the net of words I'd woven.

"Why shouldn't I simply kill you and take the diamond—along with any other treasures you possess?" He scanned the area, as if looking for my reinforcements. "You are but a lone woman, after all. Or do you expect me to believe your pet will protect you?"

I hummed a note of a song, and Efe sprang to her feet, alert and quivering. A fine line to dance with her, as I wanted her to look menacing without losing her mind. Efe had her own inner demons to battle as much as I did. I smiled, touching the spot behind her jaw to reassure her, making my own confidence clear. "The hand of Danu protects me," I replied. "I have nothing to fear from you."

He grunted. Flicked his fingers. As I'd expected him to do. I sank into the dance, drawing my sword as one of his men lunged at me. I allowed the serpent to rise, embracing her black and bitter fury, guiding her with silver bright lines. *Clear mind. Clear heart. Eyes where you want to go.* Efe would stay calm. I would kill this man, and this man only, and only if he forced me to.

It took only moments, though I retained a clarity of knowing that I hadn't before, observing as the man swung the flat of his blade to knock me unconscious. I went low, sinking beneath the swing, coming up inside it. Snap kick to the unguarded groin with the momentum of my rising. Shallow slice across his ribs with my sword. Instead of offering a pearl, I lifted my left hand and put the point of my dagger at the pulse point of his neck. The man froze and I kept my eyes on his face, contorted in fear of me, and spoke, ice in my voice. "Tell him to stand down, or I'll kill you all."

"Desist," Master Tamrat ordered. He looked at me, new respect in his eyes as the man backed away. "I accept your offer," he said, almost placatingly. "Let's document this truce."

Somewhere, if she looked down on me, I thought Kaja might be proud. Possibly my mother, too.

* * * *

I rode Efe out of the gates again, leaving my curse with the diamond behind me forever. I carried with me Master Tamrat's vow—written in blood, mainly because it amused the cruel empress in me to torment the man a little—to prevent all further attacks against their neighbors. I promised to return and take him to pieces if he failed, starting with his cock and working up. He believed that, too.

As if as an afterthought, I indicated Efe's burden, saying I brought food for relief of those affected by the floods, and inquired where I might leave them to be honorably distributed. I suggested that if Danu was pleased by the recommendation Master Tamrat gave me, then more would be sent their way. He didn't exactly respond eagerly—the plight of the common folk barely concerned him—but he brightened when I suggested other favors would come his way. I casually gave him a pearl as I spoke of it, pretending I had no idea how valuable it was.

Easy to do, as once I hadn't known. But now I did. I'd grown up a great deal in a short time. Master Tamrat's guard escorted me to a storehouse staffed with people frantically managing a long line of supplicants looking for food. The people had hollow eyes and their ribs showed through their flood-ruined clothing. Counting up the numbers for Palesa and Thanda, I resolved to help them gather and send more than what I'd brought. The people there welcomed the bounty I unloaded, though it greatly confused them. I simply told them the goddess Danu offered them Her help and suggested how they might honor Her in return. Beginning with their elephant kin.

My mother had been right, in a way. I'd learned from her and found power in what she taught me. Better, what I'd found came from me and not my family, not who I married, not who I obeyed. Thus unburdened, Efe and I left Chimto again.

Clear mind. Clear heart. Warrior, priestess, and woman. All parts of me. All one. I'd found the power to free myself, and the family I'd found. Now I would turn my gaze to building the power to free my sisters. One day, I would enter the Imperial Palace as greater than any emperor. And I would bring Danu's bright blade and unflinching justice upon them.

But not yet. The time would come. Until then I would savor all I'd hoped for.

I put eyes where I wanted them, and Efe and I headed home.

~ Epilogue ~

"Ela, Efe!" I urged. The elephant responded with liquid grace, wheeling about and meeting Capa's charge with ease. I tagged Kajala with my blunted weapon, neatly unseating her and sending her to the dust. Efe trumpeted and I cheered. Capa only wagged her head and Kajala threw me a rude gesture before scrambling to her feet.

"It's not fair that you can come around that fast," she complained.

"Nevertheless," Ochieng said sternly, "you should treat your mother with more respect."

I leaned onto my belly, hugging Efe's head. She'd grown somewhat bigger over the years, now that she ate regularly and suffered less anxiety. The same could be said of the both of us. After four children and all the years of Ochieng's diligent nurturing, I was no longer the slip of a girl I'd been when I first arrived in Nyambura. Fortunately I'd maintained my training routines and I sported as much muscle as Kaja had, so long ago. I kept myself in peak warrior condition, never forgetting that the day would come for me to keep my promises.

"Smaller can be better and faster," I reminded my daughter.

"Yes," Ochieng agreed. He helped Kajala to her feet, then came over to pat Efe, and run an affectionate caress over my calf. "But you were careless. If Kajala had paid more attention—as I expect her to do next time—she could've hit you with an arrow as you passed. Run it again."

I made a face at him, glancing at the late afternoon sun. "It's almost time for a dip in the river." I blew him a little kiss. "Or a soak in the bathing pool. If we quit now, we can beat everyone else there and have it to ourselves." At least one of our children had been conceived there, possibly more.

He gave me a long, intrigued look, eyes heating for me with desire, even after all these years together. "You make a tempting offer, but I'd like to make sure this new technique is perfect."

I had to agree. The years had been good to us, but they'd also brought others envious of our bounty. My truce with Master Tamrat had bought us a number of years. But, as Ochieng always says, we can count on things to change. New powers rose, in Chimto and elsewhere. They often turned their greedy gazes upriver and we continued to harshly disillusion them. It wasn't an ideal world, but for the most part we lived in peace and prosperity.

I couldn't help but think that Danu had a hand in bringing those tests to us, reminding me always to improve my skills. Between us, Ochieng and I, and our larger family, had amassed and refined a fighting force to be proud of. We led a coalition of free villages all up and down the river—and beyond—well trained forces ready to heed our call.

And if my sons and daughters had grown up knowing how to be warriors, then better that than being slaves. They knew their own power and how to use it to protect those without it. Now that Kajala was nearly as old as I'd been when I married the first time and our youngest, Shaharlan, had reached the age of manhood, my eyes turned often toward the setting sun, thinking of my sisters.

Lately Danu whispered in my dreams of setting the balance back to rights. The time had nearly come. I only awaited a sign.

"All right," I agreed, kicking Ochieng's hand away in mock irritation. He only grinned at me and stepped back. "Kajala, honey, mount up and—"

Efe roared, rearing up, and only long habit kept me astride. The other elephants trumpeted the same, a deafening chorus. It wasn't only Efe's dance—the ground itself seemed to undulate beneath us. Ochieng staggered, then caught himself, gaze snapping up to the sky.

I followed the direction of his gaze, gasping at the streaks of color shooting through the previously clear blue. I half-imagined shapes of winged creatures flew through the air. In the distance, thunder rolled when there should be none, so long away from the rainy season. It wasn't only the sky, however. The grasses seemed to rattle, and the river churned an unnatural shade of violet down below the lagoon.

Efe calmed, though still making querulous sounds, and I lowered my eyes to meet Ochieng's. "What was that?"

He held up his hands, palms up, and the light seemed to gather there, radiating out. He smiled slightly, delight and apprehension mingling. "That, my Ivariel, was magic returning to the land."

I gaped at him, having not at all expected that answer, and yet knowing in my heart he spoke the truth. "Magic," I echoed.

"How and why?" Kajala demanded, a dagger in her hand, her young woman's body poised to fight.

"Put your dagger away," Ochieng chided her. "I don't know how or why. Only that it has. As foretold."

I slid off of Efe and went to him. "I suppose this is the sign I've been waiting for."

He nodded, somberly. "That we've been waiting for."

"What are you two talking about?" Kajala demanded.

I glanced at her. "You know how you, your sister, and brothers have been nattering at me all these years, wanting to know about where I came from and wanting to see the world?"

She narrowed her eyes at me. "Yes…"

I cupped her cheek, all the love in my heart overflowing for her. She and her siblings possessed all my grace and agility, but none of the soft helplessness. I couldn't have been prouder.

Nodding at her dawning understanding, I kissed her forehead.

"The time has come."

About the Author

Jeffe Kennedy is an award-winning author whose works include non-fiction, poetry, short fiction, and novels. She has been a Ucross Foundation Fellow, received the Wyoming Arts Council Fellowship for Poetry, and was awarded a Frank Nelson Doubleday Memorial Award. Her essays have appeared in many publications, including *Redbook*. Her most recent works include a number of fiction series: the fantasy romance novels of *A Covenant of Thorns*; the contemporary BDSM novellas the *Facets of Passion*, and an erotic contemporary serial novel, *Master of the Opera*.

A fourth series, the fantasy trilogy *The Twelve Kingdoms*, hit the shelves in May 2014 and book one, *The Mark of the Tala*, was nominated for the RT Book of the Year. The sequel, *The Tears of the Rose,* was nominated for the RT Reviewers' Choice Best Fantasy Romance of 2014, and the third book, *The Talon of the Hawk*, won the RT Reviewers' Choice Best Fantasy Romance of 2015. Two more books follow in this world, beginning with *The Pages of the Mind* (which won the Romance Writers of America's Rita Award in 2017). A fifth series, the erotic romance trilogy, *Falling Under*, started with *Going Under*, and was followed by *Under His Touch* and *Under Contract.*

She lives in Santa Fe, New Mexico, with two Maine coon cats, plentiful free-range lizards, and a very handsome Doctor of Oriental Medicine. Jeffe can be found online at her website, JeffeKennedy.com, every Sunday at the popular Word Whores blog, on Facebook, on Goodreads, and pretty much constantly on Twitter @jeffekennedy.

Don't miss Dafne's adventure in *The Pages of the Mind...*

Magic has broken free over the Twelve Kingdoms. The population is beset by shapeshifters and portents, landscapes that migrate, uncanny allies who are not quite human...and enemies eager to take advantage of the chaos.

Dafne Mailloux is no adventurer—she's a librarian. But the High Queen trusts Dafne's ability with languages, her way of winnowing the useful facts from a dusty scroll, and even more important, the subtlety and guile that three decades under the thumb of a tyrant taught her.

Dafne never thought to need those skills again. But she accepts her duty. Until her journey drops her into the arms of a barbarian king. He speaks no tongue she knows but that of power, yet he recognizes his captive as a valuable pawn. Dafne must submit to a wedding of alliance, becoming a prisoner-queen in a court she does not understand. If she is to save herself and her country, she will have to learn to read the heart of a wild stranger. And there are more secrets written there than even Dafne could suspect...

And look for the Twelve Kingdoms trilogy that started it all!

The tales tell of three sisters, daughters of the high king. The eldest, a valiant warrior-woman, heir to the kingdom. The youngest, the sweet beauty with her Prince Charming. No one says much about the middle princess, Andromeda. Andi, the other one.

Andi doesn't mind being invisible. She enjoys the company of her horse more than court, and she has a way of blending into the shadows. Until the day she meets a strange man riding, who keeps company with wolves and ravens, who rules a land of shapeshifters and demons. A country she'd thought was no more than legend—until he claims her as its queen. In a moment everything changes: Her father, the wise king, becomes a warlord, suspicious and strategic. Whispers call her dead mother a traitor and a witch. Andi doesn't know if her own instincts can be trusted, as visions appear to her and her body begins to rebel.

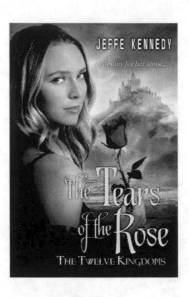

Three sisters. Motherless daughters of the high king. The eldest is the warrior-woman heir; the middle child is shy and full of witchy intuition; and the youngest, Princess Amelia, she is as beautiful as the sun and just as generous.

Ami met her Prince Charming and went away to his castle on the stormy sea-cliffs—and that should have been her happily ever after. Instead, her husband lies dead and a war rages. Her middle sister has been taken into a demon land, turned into a stranger. The priests and her father are revealing secrets and telling lies. And a power is rising in Ami, too, a power she hardly recognizes, to wield her beauty as a weapon, and her charm as a tool to deceive…

Amelia has never had to be anything but good and sweet and kind and lovely. But the chess game for the Twelve Kingdoms has swept her up in it, and she must make a gambit of her own. Can the prettiest princess become a pawn—or a queen?

Three daughters were born to High King Uorsin, in place of the son he wanted. The youngest, lovely and sweet. The middle, pretty and subtle, with an air of magic. And the eldest, the Heir. A girl grudgingly honed to leadership, not beauty, to bear the sword and honor of the king.

Ursula's loyalty is as ingrained as her straight warrior's spine. She protects the peace of the Twelve Kingdoms with sweat and blood, her sisters from threats far and near. And she protects her father to prove her worth. But she never imagined her loyalty would become an open question on palace grounds. That her father would receive her with a foreign witch at one side and a hireling captain at the other—that soldiers would look on her as a woman, not as a warrior. She also never expected to decide the destiny of her sisters, of her people, of the Twelve Kingdoms and the Thirteenth. Not with her father still on the throne and war in the air. But the choice is before her. And the Heir must lead…

Also available by Jeffe Kennedy

Fresh out of college, Christine Davis is thrilled to begin a summer internship at the prestigious Sante Fe Opera House. But on her first day, she discovers that her dream job has a dark side. Beneath the theater, ghostly music echoes through a sprawling maze of passageways. At first, Christy thinks she's hearing things. But when a tall masked man steps out of the shadows—and into her arms—she knows he's not a phantom of her imagination. What she can't deny is that he is the master of her desire. But when her predecessor—a missing intern—is found dead, Christy wonders if she's playing with fire…

Printed in the United States
by Baker & Taylor Publisher Services